Cover Design and Interior Format
© **KILLION**
GROUP, INC.

A DEWBERRY FARM

Mistletoe Murder

MYSTERY

Karen MacInerney

Books in the Dewberry Farm Mystery Series

Killer Jam
Fatal Frost
Deadly Brew
Mistletoe Murder

Dyeing Season (Coming 2018!)

Chapter 1

"I LOVE A WOODSTOVE ON A cold night," Flora Kocurek said as the wind whipped out of the north, moaning around the yellow farmhouse and rattling the windowpanes.

It was cold and raining outside, but inside, the fire was warm and bright. The Buttercup Knitting Brigade was settled around my big pine kitchen table, munching on snickerdoodles and sipping hot chocolate—some of it laced with rum. It was just a few days before Christmas, and we were all working on our Christmas gifts... none of which was quite done yet. It was a busy season for all of us; I'd been harvesting winter veggies for the Blue Onion Café and the Red and White Grocery. I'd made lots of preserves over the summer, and I was offering those along with beeswax candles, mistletoe bunches, and homemade soap for sale at weekend markets. I'd experimented with a few new products this year, including a few homemade cheeses and some lavender sachets I'd hand-stitched and stamped with the Dewberry Farm logo, but they'd already sold out. Based on the rate at which I was managing to knit, Tobias, the local vet—and my boyfriend—a scarf, though, I wouldn't be adding knitted items to my inventory anytime soon. At least not anything knitted by me.

"Supposed to ice over tonight," my friend Molly said. She pushed a strand of hair out of her eyes and inspected the red and white scarf she was knitting. "As long as we're home by midnight, though, we should be okay; temperature won't drop until then."

"I'm glad we got Bessie Mae's house fixed up last year," said Quinn, another of my friends, who was working on a stocking cap for her organic-farmer boyfriend Peter Swenson. She wore a big red Aran Islands sweater—a treat to be able to wear in Texas—and her curly hair was done up in a green ribbon. With her pink cheeks and upturned nose, she reminded me of a Christmas elf.

"I saw her down there waving to the trains just today," Flora said. "She looked happy." The proceeds of last year's Christmas Market had gone to renovating the house elderly Bessie Mae Jurecka had lived in her whole life. This year's proceeds were to go toward renovating the courthouse. What had started as a minor fix-up in November had turned into a giant nightmare when workers discovered the old wood building was being held together largely by termite spit. Although it was decorated gaily for Christmas on the outside, with garlands and lights and two big wreaths on the doors, the inside was a chaotic mess of ripped-up wood flooring and torn-out walls.

"How's the courthouse renovation going, anyway?" Molly asked Quinn, as if reading my mind.

"Slowly," Quinn said. She owned the Blue Onion Cafe, which was one of the town's gathering hubs and right across from the courthouse, so she was the source of the latest information on the doings of downtown Buttercup. "And I can't believe I forgot to tell you what they found today!"

"More wood rot?" I joked.

"Um... not exactly," Quinn said, and leaned forward over the table. "Bones."

"Bones. Well, that's festive," Molly quipped. As she spoke, there was a knock at the door; everyone jumped. I walked over to answer it; it was Serafine.

"I'm so sorry I'm late," she said as she hurried inside. "It's wicked out there tonight!"

"Come in and warm up with some hot chocolate," I suggested. "Everyone except Opal's here tonight."

"She had to pick up a shift down at the sheriff's office," Molly said as Serafine took off her raincoat and came in, rubbing her hands together. "How are the bees doing in this weather?"

"They're hunkered down, staying warm," Serafine said as I poured her a mug of hot chocolate. Serafine had opened the Honeyed Moon Mead Winery a few months back, and had several hives of bees on her property.

"A touch of rum to warm you up?"

"Oh my word, that would be just what the doctor ordered," Serafine said as she pulled a black cap with cat ears out of her knitting bag. If she ever finished it, her sister Aimee would look terrific in it. "Now. I've got to do twenty more rows in the next five days. If I get it done, it'll be a Christmas miracle."

"Hear, hear," I said, eyeing my scarf with trepidation. "How long does a scarf have to be to be functional, anyway?"

"Longer than ten inches," Quinn said with a grin.

"It's much longer than ten inches," I said. "It's like fourteen, maybe even fifteen, if I stretch it a little. Can't you make them bigger by blocking them or something?"

"Not that much bigger," she said.

I sighed and picked up the knitting needles. I'd started it last year and hadn't finished it; I was hoping this would be the year, but I might have to give it to Tobias next Christmas instead. If I got it done in time. "Tell us more about the courthouse," I said.

Serafine perked up. "The courthouse? That place gives me the creeps." She gave a theatrical shudder. "Did they find something nasty in there?"

"They found a few old paintings, but they also found something else," Quinn confirmed. "Bones."

"Like, opossum bones?" Molly asked hopefully.

"Maybe," Quinn answered. "Or maybe human."

The wind howled outside, and even though the kitchen was warm, I shivered. "Where were they?"

"They took off the skirting, and Ed Zapp's beagle got off the leash and ran under the courthouse. When they finally got him to come out, he had what looked like a femur in his mouth."

"How recent?" Molly asked quietly, taking another sip of her rum-laced hot chocolate.

"It was old," Quinn said, and we all breathed a quiet sigh of relief. "Rooster came waddling over," she said, referring to our less-than-competent sheriff, "and is theoretically running an investigation."

"Any ideas on who it might be?" I asked. "I mean, have you heard anything at the cafe? I don't expect Rooster to have come up with anything."

"Not yet," she said. "They stopped the renovation, of course. I was hoping Opal would be here to give us any juicy details."

"I invited Mandy, too," I said—Mandy Vargas being the primary reporter of the *Buttercup Zephyr*—"but she's got some family trouble going on, apparently.

Plus, she claimed not to know how to knit."

"I think maybe we need to teach her," Molly said. "How else are we supposed to stay informed?"

"You could always buy the paper," I pointed out. As a former journalist, I was a big proponent of supporting local papers.

"Of course I'm going to buy the paper," Molly said. "But I want to know *before* the paper comes out. What's going on with Mandy's family?"

"Her sister and her husband are in for a visit, and apparently, things aren't going very well."

"Are they staying with her?"

"They are," I said. "Apparently, they have a bit of a fiery relationship."

"I'm surprised she didn't come just to get out of the house," Quinn said. "That can be hard to live with." She shivered, as if shaking off memories of her violent ex. "But let's get to work, ladies. This hat isn't going to knit itself!"

The wind kicked up again outside, and we all reached for more cookies as we worked on our Christmas projects. And if there were a few snickerdoodle crumbs in the finished products? Well, it would be okay, we decided

When the group began breaking up, heading out into the cold, wet evening—I'd made another inch of progress, which meant with steady work it would bring the scarf up to a whopping nineteen inches by Christmas Day—Flora stayed behind to help me clean up. She'd been quiet that night, and as she dried the clean mugs in her slow, methodical way, I had the feeling she had something she wanted to talk to me about.

"How are things out at your place?" I asked as I scrubbed out the hot chocolate pot with some steel wool.

"Okay, I guess," she said. "But... it's kind of lonely. I think I'm the only one who doesn't have anyone to knit anything for."

"I thought you were making that blanket for your cousin's baby?" I asked.

"I have a confession to make," she said as she replaced a mug on the shelf with bony fingers. "I started that blanket fourteen and a half years ago. The baby is about to get his learner's permit."

"Ah," I said. The yarn wrappers *had* seemed kind of vintage. It made sense now. "So, the dating thing isn't going too well?"

"No, it's not," she said. "Sometimes I wonder if Roger really was my true love."

"Oh, honey." I put down the pot and looked at Flora, whose eyes looked like they were welling with tears. "He wasn't, I assure you." Although Flora had come into her own when dating her ex, he'd turned out to be a bad apple.

She swiped at her eyes. "I know that, but... this time of year is hard."

"I get that," I told her. I'd spent many Christmases without a special someone to share the holiday with. I did at least have my parents, though, and I knew Flora didn't share my good fortune. Her father had passed years earlier and her mother, Nettie Kocurek, had died not long ago. Nettie hadn't been a very nice person; in fact, she'd been a tyrant where Flora—and everyone else in Buttercup—was concerned. "Hey," I said. "I could use some help at the Christmas Market tomorrow afternoon. Would you like to come give me a hand?"

"I've never done anything like that before," she replied, her eyes darting around the room nervously.

"It'll be fun! I'll show you what to do," I assured her. "Meet me there at five, okay?"

"Are you sure?"

"Unless we get iced out, I'm positive."

She gave me a tremulous smile. "Thank you, Lucy. You just seem to know how to meet people. I've never been good at that." My rescue poodle Chuck, sensing her emotion, came over and plopped himself down on her feet. She reached down and tickled his tummy, and he writhed with pleasure.

"It'll come," I told her, surveying the clean kitchen. "Thanks so much for helping me out; and I'm so glad you came." As I spoke, a fresh wave of cold rain dashed against the windowpanes. "Now, why don't you hurry home before it gets any colder?"

"I probably should," she said, giving Chuck one more belly rub. "Thanks again, Lucy. I know we didn't get off on the right foot, what with my mother and all, but thanks for including me in the knitting group."

"My pleasure," I said, walking her to the door.

As I watched her hurry to her mother's Cadillac in the driving rain, I found myself hoping she'd find some Christmas magic of her own this year. I knew the odds of finding someone while helping me out at the Christmas Market were low, but it was better than sitting in her mother's brick ranch-style house alone.

❦

I woke the next morning buried under two down

comforters, with Chuck snuggled in next to me and a cool, wintry light filling my bedroom.

I knew I should get up and check on the livestock— before going to bed, I'd made a last round to be sure the cows and goats were tucked away safe in the barn and the chickens were all in their coop—but I lingered a moment, enjoying the light and the feel of the chilly morning air on my nose contrasted with the warmth under the comforter.

Finally, my sense of duty got the better of me, and I emerged from under the covers. Chuck just burrowed in deeper, although I knew once he heard the clatter of dishes in the kitchen, the lure of breakfast would have him running to join me. I threw on a pair of jeans, some wool socks, and a thick woolen sweater and headed toward the kitchen.

The first stop was the woodstove; I tossed in a few scraps of wood and coaxed the fire back from the embers, and then turned to the morning's next task: coffee. As I scooped the fragrant grounds into the coffeemaker, I gazed at the frozen world outside my window. The rain had turned to ice at some point during the night, leaving a wintry, ice-glazed won- derland behind. The slender branches of crape myrtle outside the kitchen window were coated in ice, weigh- ing down the tips, and the bird feeder was surrounded by fluttering, puffed-up birds. An old plum tree in the corner of the yard had suffered a broken limb from the weight of the ice, and I found myself worrying about the stately live oaks with their wide-spreading branches; how many of them had lost limbs, too?

I slipped my sock-clad feet into boots, grabbed a jacket and gloves, and headed out into the near-si- lent world. The rain gauge, though icy, showed almost two inches of rain—good news for drought-plagued Texas, and particularly for me, because my well had run dry a few months earlier—and the thermometer was hovering at just under 30. I'd planted my more tender winter veggies under hoops I'd covered with cloth; I hoped the protective cloth—and the veggies sheltering beneath it—had survived the winds. The grass crunched under my boots as I walked to the barn to let out the cows and goats, who were excited at the opportunity to explore the frozen world, and then checked on the chickens and the veggies.

The farmhouse was much warmer and redolent of coffee by the time I closed the door behind me, with two pails of milk, enough eggs for breakfast in my jacket pocket, and a sense of relief that all the living things on the farm had survived the storm. I wasn't milking much right now—Blossom, Hot Lips, and Gidget were all pregnant, so I was gradually "drying them off"—but I was hoping to have time to make another batch or two of cheese before the final day of the Christmas Market, which wasn't far away.

I fixed myself a cup of coffee, adding a bit of fresh milk before pouring the rest of it into two pots on the stove to process, then cracked a few eggs into a bowl and popped two slices of Quinn's Christmas bread into the toaster. That got Chuck's attention.

A few minutes later, as I was just sitting down to the table after splitting the eggs with Chuck, there was the sound of a vehicle coming up the drive. I recognized the truck; a moment later, Tobias appeared at the front door, smiling and waving at me through the rippled glass.

"What a nice surprise! What brings you here?" I asked when I opened the door. His dark hair was speckled with a bit of frost, and his cheeks were ruddy with the cold. He looked so handsome he literally took my breath away.

He kissed me, and I thought I might die of a heart attack right then and there. When he let me up for air, Chuck was dancing around his feet, begging for attention.

Tobias bent down to greet him. "Hi, buddy! You're full of energy this morning." He glanced up at me, a glint in his eyes. "The diet must be working."

"Right," I said, glad Chuck had already scarfed down all the evidence of the eggs I'd slipped him. At least I hadn't added cheese or bacon to them this morning.

"I've got a few more eggs from the chickens if you're hungry," I offered. "And some toast from Quinn's Christmas bread."

"I already ate," he said, "but I wouldn't say no to a cup of coffee."

"You're on," I said, feeling almost giddy as we walked into the kitchen. If you'd told me five years ago, as I slaved away in a cubicle in Houston, that I'd be waking up in my grandmother's farmhouse on a frosty morning, cooking my own eggs and entertaining a handsome and extremely diverting veterinarian boyfriend, I would have laughed.

But here I was.

"What are you up to today?" I asked as I poured him a cup of coffee and added a bit of milk from the pot on the stove.

"I'm visiting a few ranches and farms nearby, checking on some animals who had a tough time last night."

"How are the roads?"

"They're pretty good, actually. I just go slowly."

"Be careful," I warned him. "I don't want you to end

up in the hospital."

"I wouldn't drive if it wasn't safe," he reassured me. "Besides, I'm back at the clinic this afternoon with back-to-back appointments."

"I'm here until late this afternoon getting ready for the Market," I told him. I had a couple of dozen more soaps to cut and package, and I was hoping to pour another batch of beeswax candles. "Did you hear about what they found at the courthouse?" I asked.

"Old bones." He grimaced. "Sometimes I think there's too much history in this town."

"I like it," I said. Which was a good thing, because I'd signed on to renovate a historic house a few months ago. Progress had been... well... slow. I was hoping to get to it in January, budget permitting; the first bids for work had been more than I'd anticipated. "Are you coming to the Christmas Market tonight? Flora Kocurek's going to help me out at my stall."

"How did that come about?"

"I offered," I told him with a shrug. "She's lonely."

"That was nice of you," he said.

As he took another sip of coffee, the phone rang.

"Lucy? It's Quinn."

"What's up?" I asked. Her voice sounded urgent.

"Remember how we were talking about Mandy's sister being in town last night, and how she and her husband weren't getting along too well?"

"Yeah," I said.

"Well, Mandy's brother-in-law's dead."

Chapter 2

ICLUTCHED THE PHONE. "DEAD? YOU mean,
like of a heart attack or something?"

"Not exactly," Quinn said. "Somebody stabbed him
in the back right in the parking lot of Rosita's." Rosita's was the local Mexican restaurant, run by Mandy's
parents. I'd been planning to run by to pick up some
tamales in the next day or two; Mandy's mother only
made them at Christmas, and they were the best I'd
ever tasted.

"That's horrible," I told her. "Hang on a second;
Tobias is here. Let me tell him what's up." When I'd
filled him in on what Quinn had told me, I got back
on the phone. "When did it happen?"

"Last night sometime," she said. "They arrested Mandy's sister, Isabella, this morning. Apparently, Isabella
and her husband got into a huge fight last night at the
restaurant, and she stormed out of the place threaten-
ing to divorce him."

"Do you think she was the one who killed him?" I
asked.

"It's hard to say; I don't know her very well," Quinn
said. "I met her a few days ago, when she and Mandy
came in for lunch. She seemed nice. Kind of distracted,
but not the kind of person you'd expect to stab someone in the back." She sighed. "I heard her complaining

about her in-laws, though."

"Who are her in-laws?"

"The Stones. They live out toward La Grange. Own a big cattle operation. I don't think they liked Isabella very much."

"I'll bet they *really* don't like her now," I said.

"It's so sad this had to happen right before the holidays," Quinn said. "I know both families will be crushed."

"Well, if Isabella's innocent, I'll bet Mandy will find a way to prove it." As I spoke, there was the sound of a car on the gravel drive. I turned to see Mandy's car driving toward the farmhouse, way too fast. "Speaking of Mandy, guess who's here?"

"I'll let you go, then. Let me know how it goes, okay?"

"I'll call you shortly," I promised, and hung up.

"Someone stabbed him in the back?" Tobias asked as we watched Mandy park the car.

"Yes, and I'm guessing Mandy's not too happy about the way Rooster's handling the case."

As soon as Mandy got to the door, anxiety rolling off her in waves and steam practically shooting out her ears, I knew I was right.

Mandy spent the first five minutes at my kitchen table railing on Rooster Kocurek, Buttercup's sheriff, before pausing long enough to have a sip of coffee.

"When did they find his body?" I asked.

"My mother found him this morning," she said. "She was going in at six to make tamales, and there he was, in the parking lot, smelling like beer and bleeding all over the place, with a sprig of mistletoe in his hair. I'm surprised she didn't have another stroke."

"She just got out of the hospital a little while ago, didn't she?" I asked.

Mandy nodded. "That's part of the reason Isabella came to town. She and I were going to help with the tamales, take some of the pressure off her. And now this..." She ran a hand through her silky black hair and took another sip of coffee. She was so amped up, I was kind of wishing I'd made decaf.

"I'm so sorry," I said. "I know this is the last thing your family needs."

"Was the murder weapon at the scene?" Tobias asked. His father had been a cop, so he knew the ropes.

Mandy nodded. "It was one of the knives from the restaurant kitchen."

"Isabella and her husband were staying with you while they were in town, right?" I asked.

"Yes. Randy's parents were miffed about it, but Isabella wanted to be closer to our parents' house and the restaurant, so she could help out."

Tobias took another sip of coffee. "Did Randy come home last night?"

"No," Mandy said. "He likes to go to the Hitching Post and have a few beers. Or more than a few beers. Isabella and I figured he'd just gone to stay with his parents, you know, to cool off."

"Was Isabella home with you the whole night, then?"

"That's the thing," she said. "I thought she was, but there were tire tracks this morning, in the ice. Someone took out her car. She said it wasn't her, but I don't know what to believe. I know she didn't kill him, though." She looked at me with an appeal in her brown eyes. "I need to find out what happened last night. I know how good you are at finding things out, and I was hoping you could help me. If Isabella is locked up for the rest of her life for killing Randy..." Her eyes watered, and she swiped at them.

"I'll help you find out what happened," I said, and Tobias and I exchanged glances. Randy had been killed with a knife from the restaurant kitchen, and all evidence pointed to Isabella having gone out the night before, despite her denial. I'd help find out the truth, but there was no guarantee Mandy would like it.

"If there's anything I can do to help, count me in," Tobias offered.

Mandy looked relieved. "Thanks," she said, sagging into her chair.

"First question," I said. "Who else would have wanted to kill Randy Stone?"

Tobias leaned forward, elbows on the table. "Particularly anyone with access to Rosita's kitchen."

"That's part of the problem," Mandy replied. "I don't know that much about him or his friends. He and I didn't get along too well, so we kind of kept our distance. I know he liked to go drinking down at the Hitching Post, though."

"Was he an alcoholic?"

"I think so," Mandy said. "He's gone through a case of Lone Star in about two days, and that's just what he drank at the house."

"Sounds like Isabella's well out of it," I said. "Although divorce would have been preferable. Did he have any life insurance?"

"Some," Mandy said. "Which, under normal circumstances, would be great, but now..."

"More motive," Tobias supplied.

"Have you talked with the kitchen staff at Rosita's

yet?" I asked.

She shook her head. "I was hoping maybe you could come help make tamales and we could do it together, kind of under the radar."

"I've got my hands full today," I said, "but would tomorrow morning work?"

"How about nine o'clock?"

"I'll see you there," I told her.

"I should let you get on with your day," she said as she stood up to leave. "I can't thank you enough, though. I just know this had nothing to do with Isabella."

"We'll do everything we can," Tobias reassured her as she stepped out into the wintry morning. As I closed the door behind her, Tobias and I looked at each other, and I could tell we were thinking the same thing.

We were both hoping Mandy was right.

Tobias left a few minutes later, and after checking in with Quinn and putting up the milk, I spent the next hour cutting fragrant soaps, wrapping them in my handmade labels, and tying them off with raffia. When I had enough for the Market, I took a break, slipped into my boots, and went out to collect some mistletoe from the oaks by the creek.

Chuck wouldn't come any farther than the kissing gate—it was too cold and wet for him—but I happily trudged through the wheat-colored grass down to the creek, leaving a dark, wet track in my wake. The ice was melting by now, making loud, dripping noises, and although a few small branches were down, I was relieved to see no major limb damage. I gathered a few bunches of mistletoe from the oaks—with the drooping branches, it was easier to reach—and reflected on the irony of the kissing plant being both poisonous and parasitic in nature. Love could be toxic; in Randy and Isabella Stone's case, it appeared that had very much been the case. I paused before going back inside, enjoying the tang of woodsmoke on the cold air and the bleached gold fields, punctuated by the greens of live oak trees and cedars. On my way back to the farmhouse, I gathered a few cedar boughs, making sure to pick from female trees so the boughs wouldn't be loaded with yellow pollen, and added them to the wicker basket in which I'd put the mistletoe.

Back in the farmhouse, I put some beeswax into a double boiler to melt, then sorted through the mistletoe, gathering small bunches and drying them off before tying them with red velvet ribbon. They were big sellers at the Market. When I had a few dozen bunches of mistletoe ready to go, I loaded them into the basket and put them on the porch to stay chilled, then arranged the cedar boughs in the center of the table, adding a homemade beeswax candle in a jar and tucking in a few sprigs of pyracantha I'd picked down by the mailbox the day before. The red berries added a festive touch. I put on a CD of 1940s' Christmas carols, and as Bing Crosby and Frank Sinatra crooned, the smell of cedar boughs, beeswax, and woodsmoke filled my grandmother's kitchen. All I needed now was another batch of snickerdoodles—and maybe a Christmas tree.

❦

I spent the rest of the afternoon absorbed in getting

ready for the Market—it was the kind of afternoon I'd dreamed about when I worked in Houston—but the festive feeling was dampened by thoughts of the Vargas family. By the time I pulled up at the Town Square, my truck loaded with holiday goodies, the sky was darkening to deep blue, and the Christmas lights all around town were lit and sparkling.

Several of the local businesses were way ahead of me in preparation. Local artist Martin Shaw's Twin Oaks Pottery, which had opened a studio in town just a few months ago, had an amazing selection of mugs, plates, platters, and other kitchen items for sale, all in gorgeous blues, with a few greens and earthy tones mixed in. I had my eye on a big blue mug whose colors reminded me of the ocean. The Buttercup Knittery, a business I had only recently started paying attention to, was offering a selection of handmade ornaments, luscious yarns, and a selection of scarves and mittens I was planning on using as backup in the event my scarf for Tobias wasn't long enough to go around his neck. Quinn's Blue Onion stall was already loaded up with her famous Christmas bread and a variety of other yummy holiday treats, Fannie's Antiques was set up with a variety of vintage-looking Christmas decorations, and Gus Holz had already hung about a dozen of his homemade birdhouses. I had my eye on one of his bluebird houses; if I sold enough of my stock, I was getting myself one for Christmas.

Flora turned up as I finished clipping the mistletoe bundles to the front of the canopy covering my stall and stood back to admire my handiwork. I'd strung white Christmas lights and added red bows to the corners, and covered the table with a homey, festive red-and-green-plaid tablecloth. The hand-painted sign hanging from the booth said "Dewberry Farm Holiday Delights," and once I got my jams, candles, and soaps up, I hoped it would be alluring enough to draw several Market visitors.

"Hi, Flora!" I greeted her.

"It looks good," she said, nodding with approval.

"Thanks," I told her. "Could you help me get these candles out for display?" I asked. "I'll put the soaps next to them, and line up the jams on the other side."

"Sure," Flora said, looking happy to have a job. She'd dressed for the occasion in a spangled red Christmas sweater that would be a shoo-in for first place in an Ugly Christmas Sweater contest, accessorized with glowing Christmas light earrings and red lipstick that accentuated both the thinness of her lips and her skin's waxy pallor. I'd never been known for my keen fashion sense, but even I could tell she wasn't exactly dressed to kill.

Still, she was out in the world, and even if she didn't lure a potential Prince Charming, it was a lot better than being holed up at home. I watched as she placed the first few candles on the table, then got busy lining up the goat-milk soaps. I'd brought lavender, oatmeal-honey—made with honey from the Honeyed Moon Mead Winery—lemon verbena, antique rose, and a new variety I was calling Cozy Christmas, with warm spices and a touch of orange oil. I was hoping it sold like hotcakes.

By the time we managed to get everything set up, we already had customers. Many were from neighboring La Grange, but there was a good mix of locals, too, most of whom had heard about what had happened to Randy Stone and were anxious to talk about it.

"What happened to Randy Stone?" Flora asked after

the first local left. Which just went to show that she really, really needed to get out more. I knew squirrels in Buttercup who were better informed.

I gave her the lowdown on what had happened, adding that I wasn't sure Randy's wife was the culprit. I'd just finished telling her what I knew when Opal Gruber appeared with a cup of mulled mead from the Honeyed Moon Mead Winery.

"I'm so glad to see you," I told her. And then, in a lower voice, I asked, "What's going on with the Randy Stone case?"

"Not much, to be honest. It looks pretty open-and-shut. Crime of passion."

"Mandy Vargas doesn't think so," I said.

"Of course she doesn't," Opal said, giving me a sharp look over her cat-eye glasses. "Isabella's her sister. Now, I'm not sayin' it was the right thing to do, goin' after him with a butcher's knife, but that one was a bad apple through and through."

"What do you mean?"

"He got into a fight at the Hitchin' Post a few nights ago; he had trouble with liquor. And there's rumors he and his ex-girlfriend from high school were seeing each other on the sly."

"Who's his ex-girlfriend?"

"Rhonda Gehring," she said. "She's married, too. Still, those old high-school flames can be hard to put out."

Rhonda and Randy. Maybe it was a good thing they hadn't gotten together, I thought.

"I heard he was involved in the family business, too," I said. One of the locals had mentioned it while purchasing a jar of spiced pear butter.

"Couldn't hold a job, so his family took pity on him,

from what I hear," Opal said. "No wonder Isabella was fed up. I know I shouldn't say it, but I think he deserved what he got. I just wish she'd done a better job of covering her tracks."

"You think Isabella did it, don't you?"

Opal grimaced as she picked up one of my Cozy Christmas soaps. "A woman can only take so much. Oooh, these soaps smell good," she said, sniffing the soap bar. "I'll take two."

Chapter 3

MY MIND WAS CHURNING AS I wrapped up the soaps and watched as Flora counted out Opal's change. Opal might be convinced Isabella was the one who'd killed Randy, but it sounded to me like there might be some other options.

Like Rhonda Gehring. Or maybe her husband.

As Opal drifted off to the next stall, Flora was looking more disconsolate than usual.

"What's wrong?" I asked.

"Maybe I shouldn't be looking for a man," she said. "They're all scum, aren't they?"

"Some men aren't good relationship candidates," I admitted. "But then again, some women aren't either. Still, just because there are some bad eggs out there doesn't mean they're all horrible." As I spoke, Gus Holz approached the stall. "Hey, Gus," I said. "Here for some mistletoe?"

He blushed; as one of Buttercup's inveterate bachelors, I was pretty sure that wasn't on his Christmas list. He was solid, with a reddish face and only a sprinkling of gray hair around his round pate. "Nah," he said, but he darted a glance at Flora, whose right hand snuck up to fluff her hair. "I just wanted to let you know I've only got two bluebird houses left. Want me to put one aside?"

I hesitated. The Market was going well, but money was tight, and I was saving as much as I could to put toward the renovation of the old house I'd recently moved to the property. I'd gotten a windfall on a find of golden coins some time back, and the local German heritage club was contributing to the renovation, but I was still short of what I needed to finish the project. "Don't hold one for me," I told him. "If there's one left at the end of the season, I'll get it... if not, I'll just have to wait until next year."

He nodded at Flora and me, then abruptly turned away. It was an awkward moment; I wasn't quite sure what had prompted it, but when I noticed two pink spots on Flora's normally pallid cheeks, I wondered.

Had Cupid lofted a Christmas arrow while I was worrying about Mandy's sister?

Tobias arrived just as we started packing up what little was left. The Christmas lights were still glowing, and a few customers were still milling through the market, but we were pretty picked over, and I was tired.

"How was the Market?" he asked as I unclipped one of the three remaining bunches of mistletoe from the front of the stall.

"It was good," I told him, "and Flora was a godsend, but I'm worn out."

"It was fun!" Flora added, in a tone more animated than I was used to hearing from her. After I was comfortable she knew how to handle the stall, I'd taken the opportunity to wander the Market. I'd marked the scarf I had in mind—it wasn't red and white, but it was a lovely blue that would set off Tobias's eyes—and visited with Quinn and Serafine, who were both doing a booming business. Flora had done the same later on, coming back holding a bratwurst and wearing a smile that made my night.

"Up for helping out tomorrow, too?" I asked her.

"Sure!" she said, and her eyes darted across the green to the stall where Gus Holz sat surrounded by birdhouses. There was only one bluebird house left, I was disappointed to see. Ah, well...

I reached up to unclip another bunch of mistletoe, and Tobias took the opportunity to put his arms around me and land a big kiss on my forehead. I laughed and kissed him back, prompting a rogue whistle from a passerby.

"Still up for a nightcap?" he asked.

"I could use a drink," I said. "Preferably something warm, like a hot toddy." The temperature had dropped as the Market continued, and it was only a few degrees above freezing. Which was positively frigid by Texas standards.

"I'd recommend the mead, but we'll probably have a better chance of finding out more about Randy Stone if we walk over to the Hitching Post."

Once we got everything loaded up, I was more than ready for a warm drink. I set a time to meet Flora tomorrow evening and snuggled into Tobias as we walked the few blocks to Randy Stone's favorite bar.

"How was the clinic this afternoon?" I asked as we left the twinkling Christmas lights of the Square behind us. The sky was clear and studded with stars, and a half moon was riding high in the sky.

"Busy," he said. "And I had to make a few house calls tonight for folks who were worried about their livestock after last night's storm," he added. "Sometimes I wonder if it might not be time to look for a partner."

"That's one possibility," I said. "Or could you maybe trade off with another vet?"

"The thing is, the closest one is ten miles away. It's been getting busier lately, but I don't know if there's enough going on to warrant two full-time vets." He sighed. "I wish I knew someone who wanted to work part-time."

"It might be worth running an ad," I suggested. "Maybe there's a retired vet in one of the neighboring communities who'd like to keep an oar in."

"It's a thought," he said as we passed the sheriff's office. Isabella Stone was in there, I knew, probably going through Opal's back issues of *Texas Monthly* for the second time. Had she finally snapped and done in her husband? Or was something else going on?

Tobias gave me a squeeze as my eyes lingered on the small building. "We'll figure it out," he reassured me.

"I just hope she's innocent. It would tear Mandy apart if she lost her sister."

"Maybe we'll find some answers there," Tobias said, nodding toward the glowing windows of the Hitching Post, which was half a block down the street. "And if not," he said, taking my cold hand in his, "at least we can get you warmed up."

The Hitching Post was a freestanding old brick building backing the railroad tracks; the word around town was that it used to be a cotton gin. A few trucks were parked out front, and a string of old-fashioned colored lights hung from the awning. Tobias opened the door for me—it had been frosted with fake snow—and ushered me into the dark bar, which smelled of beer, must, and french fries.

There was a long wooden bar with two television

sets showing sports at the end; behind it were shelves loaded with bottles of liquor, mounted on a wall covered in old-style pressed tin. A number of saddles, bridles, and horseshoes hung on the walls at random intervals, and a poster advertising the Buttercup Rotary Club hung in the front window.

The three old-timers at the bar looked as if they'd been there so long they might have grown roots. They turned and greeted Tobias—evidently, they were all ranchers, which meant Tobias had probably been out to visit their livestock more than once—and watched as I walked up to an empty barstool, rubbing my hands together. I was the only woman there.

"Good evening, Dr. Brandt," said the bartender, a jolly-looking man in his late sixties. He turned to me with a smile. "And this is your young lady?"

It had been a while since anyone had called me a young lady, but I just smiled back and stuck out a hand. "Lucy Resnick," I told him. "I know I've seen you around, but we've never been properly introduced."

"Frank Poehler," he said, smiling a kind, genuine smile. "And these here are my regulars," he said, indicating the men at the bar. "All card-carryin' members of the Buttercup Veterinary Club."

Tobias laughed. "It's a good club."

"I'm sure glad I ain't in it anymore," said the bartender. "Thirty years is long enough. Openin' the Hitching Post was the best idea I ever had." He had the face of a man who'd spent a lot of time outside: weathered and cracked, a little like the old saddle hanging over the bar. "Haven't seen you in here in a while, Doc."

"It's been pretty busy. We were outside at the Market tonight, and I thought we'd warm her up," Tobias said.

"Can you whip up a couple of hot toddies?"

"I could, but I'm running a special on the Tom and Jerrys tonight. Try one; I promise it'll warm you right up."

"What's in it?" I asked.

"Warm milk, brandy, rum, and a little bit of egg."

"We'll take two," Tobias said, and Frank nodded approvingly. As he bustled off to make our drinks, I looked down the bar. Like Frank, the men looked like folks who had lived hardworking lives. Instead of Tom and Jerrys, two of them had Shiner longnecks, and one had what looked like the remains of a glass of whiskey.

A minute later, Frank returned with our drinks, which he set before us with a flourish. I cradled the glass mug in my hands and took a sip of the foamy concoction. Frank was right; the sweet, hot liquid seemed to light a fire in my stomach that spread out toward my chilly limbs. I took another sip. "This is dangerous!"

"They are." He nodded, pleased at my response. "My gran used to make these at Christmastime. I still love them!"

"I can see why," I told him, taking another sip.

"Slow down there, chief," Tobias said with a grin.

"I'm thinking of making you my designated driver tonight," I teased, but I put down my mug. We weren't here to get drunk on old-fashioned Christmas drinks, after all... no matter how delicious they might be.

"I hear you had a spot of trouble here last night," Tobias said.

"You can say that again," he told me. "And it didn't end well for ol' Randy Stone, either, from what I hear."

"What happened?" I asked.

"He was two out of three sheets to the wind," he

said, leaning on the bar and speaking in a low voice. It didn't matter; despite the drone of the TVs, I knew everyone else was listening. "Goin' on about the family business, how they couldn't get on without him, and a whole other load of horse... well," he added, glancing at me, "you know."

"Did someone get tired of hearing him brag?" Tobias asked.

"We're always tired of hearin' him brag," said the man next to him, taking a swig of his Shiner. "Ever hear the sayin' 'All hat and no cattle'? That was Randy Stone in a nutshell."

"I know the type." Tobias nodded.

"That wasn't what caused all the trouble, though."

"No?" I asked, taking another judicious sip of my delicious drink.

"Nope. Keith Gehring came stormin' in, wanted to know why Randy was textin' with his wife. Randy said he was full of it, but Keith had his wife's phone on him. Showed him the texts, and Randy said somethin' about blowin' things out of proportion."

"How did that go over?" Tobias asked dryly.

"It didn't go over real well, but Randy sure did," the bartender said. "Keith's got a wicked left hook. Laid him out flat on the floor, right behind where you're sittin'."

"Woulda killed him if we didn't pull him off 'im," added the guy with the Shiner.

"Wonder what was in that text," Tobias mused.

"I caught a glimpse," Frank admitted. "There were pictures, if you know what I mean, and I don't mean like photos from a Sunday church picnic. If Randy's old lady got wind of what he was up to, I can see why she'd plant a butcher knife in his back."

"It sounds like she wasn't the only one with a motive," I pointed out.

"Maybe," Frank said, "but she's the one sittin' in a cell with a stack of *Texas Monthlys* right now, so I'd put my money on her."

I wasn't so sure, but I didn't express my opinion. "Had he been in trouble here before?"

"Who, Randy?" the bartender asked. "He's been in trouble in here for years. Only reason he hasn't been as much lately is that he and the wife moved out to Katy."

"What's in Katy?" I asked.

"Well, he had a job," Frank said. "Some big-time meat sales job. Sold to the restaurant business. He was making bank, he said... woulda been a millionaire twice over if his family hadn't begged him to keep helping out with the cattle business." He all but rolled his eyes.

"So he was still working on the ranch?"

"Not on the ranch itself, at least not day-to-day," he said. "They still lived in Katy, but he came back home a lot. Said it was for work, but I never saw him workin'."

"What kind of trouble was he in before?" Tobias asked.

"Oh, he liked the ladies," Frank said. "And he liked his drink. He had wine and women down, I'll give 'im that, but he couldn't hold a tune in a bucket." The other men at the bar laughed.

"Sounds like a real gentleman," I said.

"Oh, he was a piece of work, all right. It's just too bad his old lady's gotta do time. I'd call it self-defense, if I was on that jury." He nodded at my drink, most of which I'd finished. "Can I mix you up another?"

"No, thanks," I said, covering the mug with my hand. "I've got to get back to the farm and do my chores."

"That's why I like tendin' bar better than farmin',"

Frank said. "I may have some late nights, but nobody gets upset if I miss the mornin' milkin'."

"I do miss being able to sleep in," I confessed.

"Your man doesn't spell you from time to time?" Frank asked with a wicked grin.

Tobias blushed, and I nudged him in the ribs. "Hey, that's not a bad idea. You're good with animals."

"Of course, it would be easier if you let him spend the night," he teased.

It was my turn to blush, and I noticed Tobias taking another sip of his drink out of the corner of my eye. Our relationship had been going well, but we'd both kind of drawn an unspoken line about spending the night at each other's place with any regularity.

"Looks like I touched a sore spot," Frank commented. "Sure y'all don't want another?"

"No, thanks," Tobias said. "But we'll definitely be back for more of these Tom and Jerrys."

The bartender disappeared into the back, leaving us in a bit of awkward silence. We probably should discuss the whole spending-the-night thing at some point, I thought to myself. But not now, with three men who obviously didn't have much going on in their personal lives listening.

I had finished my drink and pushed the mug away from me, thinking of suggesting we leave, when one of the regulars spoke up from beside Tobias. "There's one thing Frank didn't tell you about Randy," he said.

"Oh?" Tobias said. "What's that?"

"His old man only hired him because he told him his wife was pregnant," he said quietly. "And that if he didn't have a job, they were goin' to lose their house."

"I heard that, too," piped up another man down the bar. "I also heard his sister was fit to be tied that her daddy was letting him back in the family business."

"Why?" I asked.

"He drank down half the profits, from what I hear," he said. "He was always in line to inherit the business. Ol' William Stone's had some health problems lately, and his wife's never been much for the business. There was some talk of William handin' the reins to Randy, and his sister Jenna just about spit fire."

Now that I thought of it, I'd met Jenna at one of the weekend markets. She was trim and petite, with highlighted hair and an air of quiet confidence I remembered noting to myself was commendable, particularly in such a young woman. We'd only spoken for a few moments and, if I recalled correctly, she'd left with three bunches of fresh basil for pesto, but I'd been favorably impressed. Particularly compared to what I knew of her brother.

"I'd spit fire, too, if I was her," the grizzled man said. "She got herself an MBA out at UT, and she's got a good head on her shoulders. Randy's got an advanced degree in Lone Star and Jack Daniels. What was William thinkin'?"

"Probably that his little girl shouldn't be hangin' out around longhorns," his companion suggested.

The first man snorted. "If he thought that, he's dumber than a box of rocks."

"I won't argue that," his drinking buddy responded.

"Speaking of Jenna, any of you seen her recently?" I asked.

"She ain't what you call a regular at the Hitchin' Post," the first man said, "but she does like the huevos rancheros at Rosita's."

"I'll be over there tomorrow morning, helping the Vargases with the Christmas tamales," I said. "Maybe

I'll run into her."

"They're still makin' 'em, even with all the fuss?"

"Business is business, I guess," I said. Plus, from what Mandy had told me, the tamale trade was a big part of December's profit for the restaurant.

"Well, if you see her, tell her we're sorry for her loss," the first man said.

"And congratulations on being first in line to inherit the business," his friend added with a rueful smile

Chapter 4

"WELL, THAT WAS CERTAINLY INFORMA-TIVE," I told Tobias as we walked out of the Hitching Post back toward the Square. The Tom and Jerry *had* warmed me up; my hands were no longer like blocks of ice, and I could feel a glow in my stomach as we approached the Christmas-light-clad courthouse and the closed-up stalls of the Market. "Looks like it's not just Isabella who had a reason to take out her husband," I remarked.

"Randy wasn't a superpopular guy, that's for sure."

"Except maybe with the ladies."

"There is that," he said. "How much of what we heard is just rumor, do you think, and how much is true?"

"I usually put it at about sixty-forty, with truth being at sixty," I said. "Which part aren't you convinced about?"

"I know there was a dustup at the bar last night, and it seems pretty clear that lots of people saw what happened. I guess it's the bit about Jenna I'm wondering about. I've seen her with the animals, and she's a genuinely caring person. Some folks view their livestock as units to be sold. She understands they're beef cattle, but it's important to her that they're humanely treated... that they have good lives while they're here."

"I wish more people were like that," I commented. Some of the factory farms I'd seen had almost turned me into a vegetarian. As it was, I tried hard ensure the meat I ate came from small farms, where I knew the people raising the animals made sure they were treated well. I knew Tobias felt the same way. "I just don't know if I can imagine her killing her brother in cold blood," he said.

"So that's forty percent," I said. "What did you think about the guy who took him out with a left hook, or his wife?"

"Keith and Rhonda Gehring? I can see why Keith would go after Randy, but if Rhonda was in love with him, why would she kill him?"

"Maybe because Randy got sloppy," I suggested. "If Keith was that violent with Randy, it's possible things at home got pretty dangerous for Rhonda, too." I thought of Quinn and her abusive ex. It happened more often than I liked to think, even in a sweet little place like Buttercup.

"It's all speculation at this point anyway," he said. "It would be good to check in with the Stone family, though."

"Have any appointments out there in the near future?" I asked as we walked around to the front of the courthouse and sat down on a wrought-iron bench. The metal was cold against my jean-clad legs, and I found myself wishing I had another Tom and Jerry. Instead, I just snuggled into Tobias.

"It's about time to do a routine checkup," he said. "Maybe I'll call to see if I can come out this week."

"Can I come, too?"

"I'd love it if you did," he said, putting an arm around me. The closeness dispelled the awkwardness that had come between us earlier. Most of it, anyway. "Let's sit here a little while longer. I don't know about you, but I'm not quite ready to drive yet."

"Me neither," I said. "Those Tom and Jerrys are pretty strong." I looked at the courthouse, and the small pile of splintered wood tucked behind one of the pots of greenery flanking the front steps. "I forgot to ask about the bones," I realized.

"The bones?"

"The ones they found under the courthouse."

"Oh. I'd almost forgotten about those, with everything else going on."

"I'm sure Rooster has by now, too," I said. "Although he thinks he's got the Randy Stone case all wrapped up, so maybe not."

"This close to Christmas?" Tobias asked. "He's probably spending as much time as possible on his deer lease with his buddies and a couple of cases of Lone Star."

Which sounded like a potentially lethal combination to me, but Rooster had made it this far, so who was I to argue?

As we sat, there was the sound of squealing tires, and an ancient orange pickup truck lurched into the square. I could hear angry voices—both a man's and a woman's—and then the driver punched the gas, peeling out.

"They're going to hit the Market!" I said, just as the front left bumper clipped the bratwurst stand, sending the grill—and the hot coals in it—spinning across the parking lot. As the orange coals tumbled out across the pavement, the truck slewed to the left and then clipped another curb, coming to a screeching stop. The passenger door swung open, and a woman practically tumbled out. She didn't even have a chance to close the door before the truck driver gunned the engine and rocketed down the road toward the railroad tracks. I hoped Bessie Mae Jurecka was safe at home, and not on the streets.

Tobias and I leaped up from the bench and hurried over to where the truck's passenger was standing, hugging herself.

"It's Rhonda Gehring," Tobias said quietly.

"Randy Stone's affair partner?"

He murmured assent.

"Are you okay?" he asked as we hurried across the Square.

"I'm fine," she said, and then her face crumpled. "No, that's wrong. I'm not fine at all," she said, and burst into tears.

Instinctively, I put my arms around her, and she clung to me like she was drowning and I was a life preserver. "I've made a huge mess of everything," she bawled, and I could smell the liquor on her breath. Evidently, alcohol sales were up in Buttercup this winter. "I fell in love with the wrong man," she wailed, "and now he's dead, and I've lost him, and I love my husband, too, and I'm losing him, and there's nothing I can do about it."

"What happened in the truck?" Tobias asked.

Rhonda let go of me, as if trying to get herself together, and swiped at the mascara that was running down her face. Her eyes were big and brown, and she had pale porcelain skin that was blotchy from crying. She was pretty, and looked all of about twelve years old at the moment, although I'd put her at at least twenty-five. "Keith and I were arguing," she said. "He was furious.... I've never seen him that mad before. He just stopped the truck and told me to get out." She sniffled.

"And now I don't know if I can even go home. What will I do?"

Tobias and I exchanged glances. "It might not be a bad idea to stay somewhere other than home," I suggested.

"I don't have a wallet. I don't have anything," she said, her voice quavering. "Not even a jacket."

"We'll cover it," I volunteered. I wasn't comfortable inviting her back to my place to stay, so I followed my instinct. Funds might be tight, but I didn't want to leave her out in the cold. "Let's start heading that way," I said, and guided her across the Square to the inn.

"This has been the worst week ever," she said, sobbing.

"I heard a little bit about what happened," I told her. "Did this all go down yesterday?"

She nodded. "I left my phone on the kitchen table when I went upstairs to change my jeans—I spilled tomato sauce all over them—and when I got back downstairs, Keith had my phone in his hand." She bit her lip and blushed. "There were pictures."

Even though I already knew that, I winced. "Sounds like a rough week," I said.

"And Randy's gone... his wife killed him, all because of me. I feel so horrible!" There was a fresh wave of tears, and Tobias and I looked at each other.

We were close to the bench where he and I had been sitting when we spotted the truck. "Why don't you sit down here for a moment?" I said. "Tobias and I need a moment."

"You can wear my jacket," Tobias said gallantly. She accepted it, her slight frame swallowed by the warm down coat.

"What should we do?" I asked him when we were

a few steps away. "I'm not sure it's a good idea to leave her alone at the inn. She's pretty upset."

"Let's take her back to your place," he suggested. After a moment, he said, "I'll stay, too."

"Are you sure?" I blurted out.

"Unless you don't want me to," he said quickly.

"No, no... I do want you to," I assured him. "That would be terrific."

He sighed and looked back at her. "I think I'm okay to drive in a few minutes. Let's move your stuff to the back of my truck, and we'll come back and get your truck in the morning. That way if I have an emergency call, I'll have everything on hand."

"Do you need to stop by your place?"

He shook his head. He spent so much time away from home, taking care of other people's animals, that he'd told me he didn't feel right adopting a pet of his own. He didn't want it to be lonely. I was of the opinion that a nice clinic cat would be a good addition but hadn't broached the subject yet. Maybe that would be my Christmas present to him, I thought. It wasn't kitten season, but I was still betting it would be easier to find a kitten at the La Grange shelter than finish knitting a scarf in the next few days.

"Are you okay going back to Lucy's place and staying there?" Tobias asked Rhonda.

She nodded. "If it's not too much trouble..."

"It's not," I said. "I'm not good to drive yet, but if you'll help us move my stock over to Tobias's truck, he'll drive."

"Okay," she said in a little-girl voice. Tobias pulled up next to my truck, and we transferred everything over in just a few minutes. Before long, we were on the road to Dewberry Farm.

"This place is cute," Rhonda said as we bumped up the drive to the little farmhouse. I'd left the kitchen light on, and the house glowed welcomingly. I smiled at the sight of it. I'd spent so much time here as a child that the place was imprinted on me somehow. It felt, deep in my bones, like home.

A cold wind blew from the north as we got out of the truck, and I looked up at the sweep of the Milky Way across the dark, star-studded sky. It was going to be another cold night; I'd need to make sure the animals were warm and cozy in the barn.

Chuck greeted us at the front door, yipping as if we'd left him for a week. "Hey, buddy!" Tobias said, squatting down to give him a good scratch behind the ears. Once he'd greeted Tobias and me properly, Chuck threw himself at Rhonda, who jumped back as if he'd bitten her.

"I'm scared of dogs," she confessed.

"Chuck won't hurt you. He might love you to death, but that's about it," Tobias reassured her as I called Chuck over with a treat. We spent a few minutes taking care of Chuck's dinner requirements—no extra treats with Tobias around, much to the poodle's dismay—stoking the woodstove, and getting Rhonda settled in the bedroom above the kitchen. Then Tobias helped me unload the truck and walked to the barn with me to check on the animals and do the milking. I usually enjoyed the rhythm of farm chores alone, but it was very companionable having Tobias with me, and I had to admit things got done faster.

By the time we headed back to the farmhouse with the evening's milk, it was almost eleven. The last remnants of the Tom and Jerry had worn off, and I was chilled again. I put the milk in the fridge—I'd sterilize it with tomorrow's milk—and headed upstairs to knock on Rhonda's door. "You doing okay?" I asked.

"Fine," she said, cracking the door open. "Thanks again for having me over." She sounded sad, but not like she was going to throw herself out the window, thankfully.

"We'll head back into town by nine," I said. "Breakfast at around eight-thirty?"

"Sure. Thanks again for letting me stay."

"No problem," I said. "Sleep well."

I padded back down the stairs to the kitchen, where Tobias was warming his feet by the woodstove.

"Rhonda okay?"

"Seems so," I said. "I hope you don't mind, but I'm beat. I think I need to go to bed."

"Me too," he said. "I'm glad I don't have any appointments until ten. Let's just hope we don't have any emergency calls tonight." He stood up and put an arm around me, and any awkwardness I was afraid might come up failed to materialize at all. He gave me a soft kiss on the top of my head, and as we walked back toward my bedroom, Chuck followed us, wagging his tail. I wasn't the only one feeling good about having Tobias stay the night.

The next morning dawned cold and clear. The last of the ice had melted away from the branches, but when I let Chuck out to water the roses, the grass was frosted white in places, as if Jack Frost had tiptoed through Buttercup.

Tobias and I had slept in each other's arms all night, with Chuck tucked in between our feet. It was nicer than I could have imagined waking up with my head on his chest, warm and cozy under the duvet. I woke up at seven, but lingered until almost eight, when I knew I had to get moving. I had to get my chores done and then pick up my car before heading to Rosita's, after all. "I'll make coffee," I'd told Tobias, kissing him before slipping out of bed and into my not-very-sexy fluffy bathrobe. If you were dating a farm girl, you had to keep your wardrobe expectations reasonable.

I started the coffee and stoked the woodstove, then pulled on my rubber boots—a perfect complement to the robe—and hurried out into the cold morning to see if the chickens had provided eggs for breakfast. Although laying had slowed down now that the days were shorter, I still got a few, and I was pleased to discover five this morning; with what I had left over in the fridge, we had plenty for breakfast for three.

When I got back to the farmhouse, Tobias was in the kitchen. He looked me up and down and waggled his eyebrows. "Nice ensemble," he said. "Victoria's Secret?"

"Very secret," I replied. "Not even available in stores."

"I can't think why," he told me. "Although you look good in anything. Or nothing," he added in a provocative tone of voice.

I blushed. "Rhonda's right upstairs!"

"Have you heard from her yet?"

"I told her I'd wake her at eight," I told him. "If you'll do the honors on the eggs," I said, "I'll take care of the morning milking."

"In that?"

"I'm sure the cows won't complain," I said, "but I'll

probably switch to jeans. I don't like dragging the ends of my bathrobe in the mud." I poured two cups of coffee before heading to the bedroom to pull on a pair of jeans. By the time I got back to the kitchen, Tobias was pulling a skillet out of the cabinet, with Chuck sitting about two feet away from him, looking hopeful. I smiled to myself; his odds of getting a treat out of Dr. Brandt were slim to none.

"Fried, or scrambled?" he asked.

"Over easy for me, please," I told him. "If I'm not back, would you wake Rhonda up at eight-fifteen?"

"I will," he said as I headed out to do my chores, much to the relief of Blossom and the goats, who were anxiously awaiting their morning snack.

By the time I finished taking care of everything around the farm, it was just before eight. The kitchen smelled of coffee and woodsmoke and butter sizzling. My stomach grumbled as I set down the milk pails and pulled off my boots. "No word from Rhonda yet?"

He shook his head. "How do you think she likes her eggs?"

"I'll go find out," I told him.

But I didn't find out. Because when I got to the top of the stairs, Rhonda's door was ajar, and the bed was mussed, but Rhonda was nowhere to be found.

Chapter 5

"SHE'S NOT HERE," I CALLED down to Tobias. "Are you sure she didn't come down while I was out?"

"I've been in the kitchen the whole time," he said. "Unless she flew out the window, I would have seen her."

Remembering her frame of mind the night before, I actually did check the window, but it was closed. The bed was rumpled and the sheets pulled back; it looked like she'd slept there, or at least lain down.

But where had she gone?"

I hurried back downstairs. "I wonder when she left."

"Is the truck still here?" Tobias asked.

"It is," I answered as I stepped out onto the front porch. Frost rimed the wood slats, and the grass poking up through the pavers on the pathway, but there was no sign of footsteps. I hadn't seen footsteps in the grass when I went out the kitchen door, either—although I hadn't really been looking. I walked down the front path, scanning the grass around me for tracks, but there was nothing. It looked like Rhonda either had flown, or left well before morning. I headed back into the house, where Tobias was looking at me with concern. "If she left, it was hours ago, I'm guessing. The frost on the grass is undisturbed."

"But where would she have gone? And why?" he asked.

"Maybe she had second thoughts and called her husband," I suggested. "Maybe he came and picked her up."

"But we would have heard that," he objected. "And Chuck would have barked, wouldn't he? He's a pretty good guard dog."

"He is," I agreed, a little worm of worry in my stomach. "Wherever she is, I hope she's okay."

"Do you know Keith Gehring's number?" he asked.

"No, and I wouldn't call if I did," I said, thinking it might not be a good idea to tell a potentially violent man I'd sheltered his wife. Both for Rhonda, if she came back, and for me. "Opal would be able to get in touch with him, though."

"Good thinking. I know you need to get to Rosita's; I'll call while you go get ready."

"Thanks," I told him, and he picked up his phone while I headed back to the bedroom to finish getting dressed.

We did a last search around the house and barn, but turned up no sign of Rhonda.

"Where could she be?" I asked as I climbed into Tobias's truck. He hadn't had any calls last night, thankfully, but I knew he had a busy day ahead of him today.

"Maybe she had another friend and he or she came to pick her up," Tobias suggested as he maneuvered the truck around and headed down my long driveway. No tire tracks there, either, I noticed—not that you'd really be able to tell. The frost was starting to disappear where the morning sun kissed it, but there were still swaths of ice crystals in the shadows. It was a beautiful morning, with a clear blue sky. A cardinal swooped in front of the truck as we reached the end of the driveway.

"The thing is," I said, still thinking about Rhonda, "if anyone drove up to the farmhouse, surely we would have noticed. Chuck would have, at least."

"It's a mystery," he conceded as he turned onto the road, then voiced what we were both worried about. "I sure hope she's okay."

"Me too."

We drove in silence on the way to town. He reached over to hold my hand, and I leaned against his shoulder, thankful to be with him. It had been nice having him at the house the night before. Nice waking up next to him, nice sharing breakfast. He'd cooked, so I did the dishes: a companionable division of labor.

The drive, alas, was over too soon. "I told Opal about Rhonda," he said as he pulled in next to my truck, which was parked by the courthouse. "She said she'd pass it on."

"Good."

"She said she'd call if she found anything out. I'll text you if I hear." He leaned over and kissed me, and I felt myself relax a little bit. "Thanks for having me over last night," he said with a smile that made my heart accelerate. "It was good. I loved waking up in your arms."

"Me too," I told him, feeling warmth flush through me despite the cold. "And thanks for breakfast."

"Let's do that again soon," he suggested.

"I'd like that." I thought of Christmas, just a few days away. We'd never made any official plans; he'd met my parents, but I still hadn't met any of his family members. Was it time yet? I hadn't had the courage to broach the subject. My friend Molly had invited me to spend the day with her husband and four children at their farmhouse, but I was really hoping to spend it with Tobias. The group was planning to meet that afternoon at Molly's; maybe I'd ask for advice then.

I hopped out of the truck, still feeling a swirl of warm feelings for Tobias, uncertainty about Christmas, and downright worry for Rhonda, and waved as Tobias headed off for the clinic.

Rosita's was doing a booming breakfast business when I pulled into the parking lot just after nine. I'd like to think it was because of their breakfast tacos, which they served with a delicious creamy green jalapeño sauce that would knock your socks off and have you coming back for more five minutes later, but I suspected it had more to do with Buttercup's very active grapevine.

"I'm so glad you're here," Mandy said when I ducked into the kitchen, past a horde of gossiping locals. I'd heard the words *knife*, *parking lot*, and *girlfriend* on the way, and could only imagine how it must be for Mandy's poor family.

"How are you doing?" I asked.

"I've been better," she said. She looked tired, with her normally shiny hair pulled back in a messy ponytail and dark circles under her almond-shaped eyes. "My family won't even come to the restaurant. I've been trying to keep the restaurant and the *Zephyr* going at the same time. It was hard enough when I had Isabella helping, but now..."

"We'll get her out," I said with more confidence than

I felt. In the kitchen, the line cooks were frantically cooking eggs and warming tortillas, trying to keep up with the press out front, and Mandy had just opened another vat of her grandmother's famous green salsa and was filling little plastic cups for to-go orders.

"Are you sure you just need help with the tamales?" I asked.

"No, but that's what we're going to do," she said, fitting a last lid on a cup and then wiping her hands before drawing me toward a relatively quiet corner in the back of the kitchen. The cooks, busy though they were, stole a few curious glances. I wondered what rumors were floating around that Mandy didn't know about.

"Did you find out anything else?" she asked in a low voice, glancing around to make sure nobody was listening.

"A few things," I told her quietly. "Randy Stone wasn't a very popular guy."

"What did you find out?"

"Well, you know about his girlfriend and her husband, of course," I said. "But he apparently wasn't a terrific businessman, either, and there may have been some bad blood between Randy and his sister."

"That's some useful news," she said, perking up a bit. Despite her fatigue, she had the intense look of a reporter on the trail of a good story.

"Maybe," I conceded. "And in the interest of full disclosure, I have to tell you that Rhonda spent the night at the farmhouse last night."

She blinked. "Randy's girlfriend spent the night at your place?"

"Her husband abandoned her on the Square after taking out one of the stalls with his truck, and she needed a place to stay. The thing is, though, she left sometime during the night. And we have no idea where she went."

"Strange. Did she have a car?"

I shook my head. "And we didn't hear anyone come to pick her up, either." My stomach tightened a bit, and I wondered if Opal had gotten in touch with Rhonda's husband yet. I checked my phone, but there were no texts or calls. "I hope she's okay."

Mandy pulled a face. "I don't like her, I won't lie about that, but I'm with you. I hope no harm came to her." She paused for a moment. "Do you think maybe her husband was the one who killed Randy?"

"I don't know," I said. "The problem is, if the knife came from here, how did he get in?" And why, if Isabella theoretically stayed home the night her husband died, were there tire tracks in her driveway?

"Maybe someone left a door unlocked," Mandy suggested, looking hopeful and almost a little bit excited. "Or maybe it wasn't one of the knives from our kitchen after all. I mean, I'm sure this isn't the only place in the world you can pick up a Henckels knife."

"I don't know how common they are," I said, "but it's worth looking in to."

She sighed. "I guess we should finish making the tamales. I really appreciate you coming to help; as you can tell, we're slammed."

"I've always wanted to make them," I said.

"You won't get to see the whole process, I'm afraid. We made the fillings yesterday, so we just need to wrap them and steam them," she said, leading me to a corner of the kitchen, where there were two enormous bowls, one filled with yellow masa—the corn-flour and lard-based dough that was a staple in any tamale—and the other loaded with shredded beef. I'd eaten tons of tamales; the softened corn husks filled with masa and a spicy filling, usually meat, were a traditional Christmas dish in Mexico, but I'd never made them before. I was looking forward to learning how.

"Where are the husks?" I asked.

"I prepped them last night; they've been soaking. They should be nice and soft," she said, grabbing a bleached husk from a bucket from a nearby counter. "So, this is how it works," she said, taking a softened husk and laying it flat on a cutting board. "You spread on a couple tablespoons of the dough," she instructed me, using a spoon to spread some of the masa. "Not too thick, though, and leave about four inches of room. Then you put a few spoonfuls of the filling down the center, like this." I watched as she spread some of the spicy shredded beef over the masa. "And now, you fold it like this," she said, going through a series of folds that took only a few seconds, but looked as complex as an origami crane. "Voilà!" she said, leaving a perfectly folded tamale on the counter.

"Umm..." I said. "Are you sure you don't need someone to mix more masa, or another filling instead?"

She laughed. "It's easy once you get the hang of it."

"Right," I said, unconvinced.

"Practice makes perfect," she said. "Time to start practicing!"

By the time eleven o'clock rolled around, we'd made hundreds of tamales. Mandy made them three times as quickly and at least twice as neatly as I did, but I was getting better. I watched as Mandy filled the last husk and set it with the others, then peeled off her gloves and washed her hands.

"What now?" I asked.

"We'll steam them in batches," she said. "The hard part's done; thank you so much."

"My pleasure," I told her. "That beef filling looks delicious. What's in it?"

"Beef, spices... and peppers, of course. We make beef, pork, chicken, and bean tamales. If you like, I'll give you the recipes, but you can't tell anyone I gave them to you; they're a family secret."

"Really? I'd love that," I said.

"Now that you know how to fold them, you can have your own Mexican Christmas. Just a little bit of cinnamon hot chocolate and some salsa, and you're done!"

"Can I have the recipe for the salsa, too?"

"That I can't give you," Mandy said. "I don't even know it! My mother promises she'll leave it to us in her will." Her smile sagged, as suddenly everything that had gone wrong came back to her. Her mother was sick and her sister was in jail; so far, it hadn't been a very happy holiday season for the Vargas family. "Think they'll let me take tamales to Isabella?"

"Talk to Opal," I suggested. "She'll make it happen." Speaking of Opal, I realized I hadn't heard from her yet. I glanced at my watch; I had the Buttercup knitters in a couple of hours, and I still had some work to do to get ready for tonight's Christmas Market. I was about to tell Mandy I had to run when one of the servers from the front came looking for her.

"I'll be right back," Mandy said. "Could you put those in a clean container and in the fridge?" she asked, gesturing to a stack of white food storage containers stacked on a shelf. "There's a pen right there for the time and date."

"Got it," I said, grabbing two large white plastic containers and loading them with the tamales, being careful not to let them fall apart as I transferred them.

I had almost filled the first bucket when a petite young woman with dark eyes drifted over to me.

"Hi," I said.

"You want to know what happened to Randy, don't you?" she asked bluntly.

"I do," I said.

She glanced over her shoulder; looking for Mandy, I presumed. "Isabella came back that night," she whispered. "She took the cash out of the drawer... I think she was afraid if she didn't, Randy would come and steal it. He borrowed the key sometimes."

"So she was here that night?"

She nodded. "I had just left after finishing clearing up. I don't think they saw me; I was in my car over there at the back of the parking lot."

"What were you doing in the parking lot?"

Her eyes darted away for a moment, then back to me. "My sister called," she explained. "I don't like to talk on the phone while I'm driving."

Something told me she wasn't telling me the whole truth, but I let it go for now; I wanted to hear what she had to say. "Got it," I told her. "What happened?"

"She drove up after midnight and parked by the door. She let herself in... She was in there for like, ten minutes or so."

"Was she carrying anything when she came out?'

The young woman shook her head. "Not that I saw, but she had a big coat on. She was about to get in the car when her husband pulled into the lot."

"Really?"

"Oh, yes," she said, and her eyes grew round. She glanced over her shoulder. "They screamed at each other. She actually threw something at him. I thought she was going to hit him."

That didn't bode well for the Vargas family, I thought. "What did she throw?"

She shrugged. "I didn't see. She got into her car and drove off. And then he went into the restaurant."

"What happened then?"

"I don't know," she said. "I waited... I mean, I was on the phone with my sister for a few more minutes, but it was getting cold, so I went home."

"But Isabella left before he went into the restaurant?"

She nodded. "She did. She went toward town," she told me.

That wasn't particularly helpful news, either, because from what Mandy had told me, Isabella lived in the other direction.

"Did anyone else show up while you were here?"

"No," she said. "But about Randy..." She hesitated.

"What about him?"

Before she could answer, Mandy bustled back in. She spotted the young woman talking to me, and her brow wrinkled. The young woman scuttled away, ducking her head. "What were you and Julie talking about?" she asked.

Julie shot me a desperate look. "She was just helping me," I said, not entirely untruthfully. "Everything okay up in the front of the house?"

"Fine," Mandy said, but I could tell she wasn't buying my easy explanation. Her eyes moved from me to Julie, and then back again. "Thanks for helping me out today," she said. "Want to take a few tamales with you?"

"I'd love it," I said.

"I'll fill up a to-go container for you," she offered, "and a tub of salsa. Just steam them till they're heated up, and you're ready to go."

"Thanks," I said. "Maybe I'll invite Tobias over to share. Are you coming to knitting at Molly's today?"

"I wish I could, but with everything going on..." She waved her hand at the busy kitchen. "I should probably go to the paper and finish getting this week's issue going." She grimaced. "I hate having to write that my sister's in jail."

"Maybe there'll be someone different in jail by the time it goes to press," I suggested.

"I hope so," she said. As she handed me the to-go box and the tub of salsa, she gave me an intent look. "You'll let me know if you find anything out, won't you?"

"I will," I confirmed.

"Even if you think I won't like it?"

"Even if I think you won't like it," I agreed. Although, in this case, I was going to do a little more digging before I told Mandy what Julie had shared with me. My gut told me it wasn't yet time to share, and I had learned to trust my gut.

Chapter 6

I BARELY HAD TIME TO PUT the tamales in the fridge and let Chuck out before it was time for the Buttercup Knitting Brigade. I'd hoped to have time to make a few more candles, but I'd stayed at Rosita's longer than I'd expected; the stock I had would have to be enough. I was down to only six bundles of mistletoe, though, so I took a few minutes to head down to the oaks by the creek, using a sharp knife to cut the green shoots off the trees. I didn't feel too bad about it—it was a parasitic plant, after all, even if the Druids did think it was a magical remnant of lightning strikes—but I did start wondering about the sprig of mistletoe in Randy's hair. Where had he picked it up? Was it one of the sprigs I'd cut? I tried to remember who all had bought bunches at my stall, but there were too many to recall. Had he come back from another assignation... possibly with someone other than Rhonda? Was it possible Isabella had killed him after all?

Julie had said Isabella left before Randy did... but was she telling the truth? And why tell me any of what she'd seen at all? I wished Mandy had stayed up front a minute or two longer, so Julie had had the chance to tell me everything she knew about Randy. Maybe I'd swing by to see if I could get her alone again for a moment.

Speaking of Rhonda, I still had no idea what had happened to her, I thought as I tramped back to the farmhouse with my basket full of green mistletoe, the berries gleaming in the bright sunshine. When I got there, I set the basket on the table and picked up the phone. One of the deputies answered at the police station, so I called Opal's cell, but she didn't pick up. I left a message for her to see if she'd heard anything about Rhonda, and then called Tobias's cell. He wasn't answering either; he was probably with a client.

Feeling unsettled and confused, both by Rhonda's disappearance and what Julie had shared with me at the restaurant, I quickly tied the mistletoe into bundles and put them in the shade of the porch, where they'd stay cool, then gathered my knitting supplies and headed back out to the truck. I'd pretty much given up hope on ever finishing the scarf in time for Christmas, but I was hoping somebody had turned up some information that might help.

It was a short drive to the Kramers' ranch, and when I got there, Flora's truck was already parked; everyone I knew in Buttercup, it seemed, drove a truck.

"Come in, come in!" Molly called when I knocked on the door. I opened it, and a rush of ginger-, cinnamon-, and clove-scented air wafted over me. I inhaled, feeling 10 percent calmer already, and stepped through the front door, where I was greeted by Molly's enormous lab, Barkley.

Flora and Molly were already sitting at the big kitchen table. There was a pile of gingerbread cookies on a plate in the middle of the table, and what looked like mugs of mulled cider. "Away in a Manger" was playing in the background, and despite the fact that it was the middle of the day, Molly had lit one of my beeswax candles, lending a honeyed scent to the already delicious-smelling air.

"This place is heaven," I said.

"Wait three hours for the kids to get home," Molly said with a wry smile, "and you might have a different opinion."

I laughed. Molly's four kids were terrific, but like all teens and preteens, they could be a handful.

Flora didn't say anything, but I noticed she was wearing a dress today, a red plaid number that reminded me of a Christmas tree skirt I'd once owned, and bright red lipstick to match. "You look nice," I told her.

"Thanks," she said. "I'm looking forward to helping out again tonight at the Market."

"Somebody has a date afterward," Molly said with a mischievous grin. Flora's cheeks turned as bright as her lips, and she ducked her head.

"A date? With whom?" I asked, although I had my suspicions.

"Gus Holz," she muttered, blushing. "I'm going to help him tidy up at the end, and then we're going to go to the Hitching Post and have a drink."

"That's wonderful!" I said. "He's a nice man. Did he ask you last night, at the Market?"

"I saw him at the Red and White today. We were both looking at the apples," she told me. "He asked if I was going to be at the Market tonight. I told him I was, and he... well, he suggested we go get a drink afterward." She looked down at her outfit. "Is this okay? I had no idea what to wear."

"It's fine," I told her. "You look lovely. And if you go to the Hitching Post," I said, "try a Tom and Jerry. Tobias and I had one the other night; it's Frank's grandmother's recipe, and it's delicious."

"Do you think it's proper for a lady to drink on a first date?"

"We're in the twenty-first century, darlin'," Molly told her.

She still looked nervous. She was pulling the yarn so tight, her stitches were the size of sesame seeds; I resisted the urge to tell her to relax. "What if he turns out to be like Roger?" she asked.

"I've known Gus for years," Molly reassured her. "He's a good man; I've seen nothing to suggest his character is anything but solid. And you're just going to get a drink," she reminded her. "You're not walking down the aisle with him."

"The aisle," Flora said. "I never thought I'd get married. And then, with Roger..." Tears filled her eyes.

"He wasn't a good guy," I said. "We all have to kiss a few frogs. I know I did, anyway."

"Oh, I kissed more than I care to remember," Molly volunteered.

"Just take it slow," I suggested. "See if you enjoy his company. You can set the pace."

"But I like him," she said. "I like him so much! And I just don't want to make a mistake!"

"You'll be fine," Molly said. As she spoke, there was a knock at the door. Barkley let out an enormous woof and went to greet the new visitor; Molly followed her.

"I'm scared," Flora confessed when she'd left the kitchen.

"It's okay to be scared," I said.

"Maybe I should say no," she said. "Maybe you could tell him I'm sick."

I shook my head. "Go. I can tell you like him, and he likes you. What do you have to lose?"

Before she could answer, Opal walked in, carrying

an enormous knitting bag and looking grim. "I was hoping you'd be here," she said.

"Did you find anything out?" I asked. Molly and Flora looked at me, and then Opal.

She shook her head. "Not a word."

"What's going on?" Molly asked.

"We took Rhonda Gehring home to stay with us last night—she had a bit of a falling-out with her husband," I told them, omitting a few details, like the affair with Randy Stone. "But when we woke up this morning, she was gone."

"Weird," Molly said, looking concerned. "Do you think she's okay?"

"I don't know," I said, and looked at Opal. "Did you talk to her husband?"

She shook her head. "I even drove out there. Nobody home."

"Was his truck there?"

"No," she said.

"I know Keith works out toward La Grange, so it could be he's there today."

"Where does Rhonda work?" I asked.

"At a hairdresser's in La Grange. Shear Perfection, I think it's called," Molly said.

I picked up my phone and Googled it, then dialed. A woman with a smooth voice picked up.

"Hi," I said. "Does Rhonda Gehring cut hair for you?"

"She does," the woman confirmed. "Would you like an appointment?"

"Is she there today?" I asked.

"No," she said. "But she should be in tomorrow."

"What time?" I asked.

"She works twelve to six," she said. "I could fit you

in at one..."

"Drat," I said. "I'm crazy busy tomorrow, but maybe I'll drop in if I have time."

"She should be here the next two days, too, if you'd like me to schedule you."

"Thanks," I said. "Let me check my calendar and call you back."

"Smooth," Molly said when I hung up.

"All those years of investigative reporting," I told her. I hated misrepresenting myself, and tried very hard to avoid outright lies, but sometimes the sin of omission couldn't be avoided. Besides, it was for a good cause. "If we haven't heard from her, I'm swinging by tomorrow."

"What happened between Rhonda and her husband?" Flora asked.

Molly and I exchanged looks. "Marital troubles," I said.

"Who else is coming?" Molly asked, to change the subject. "I know Serafine is in Houston with her sister today, but is Mandy going to make it?"

"I doubt it," I said. "With everything going on, she's got her hands full. I went down to Rosita's to help make tamales today. They're slammed."

"Well, I'm glad business is good," Molly said. "It could have gone the other way."

"No chance to pick up gossip if you don't stop in for a bite," Opal pointed out.

"Does Rooster know Rhonda's gone yet?" I asked Opal.

She shook her head. "Haven't seen him. I told Deputy Shames, though. She said there was an incident at the Gehrings' a few months ago. Rhonda called, asked for an officer to come out."

"Why?"

"Argument with her husband. The deputy didn't go into details, and I didn't see the police report."

"Keith Gehring hauled off and socked it to Randy Stone at the Hitching Post the night Randy died. He's got a bit of a temper. Is Rooster still investigating other options as far as the murder's concerned?"

Opal rolled her eyes. "Rooster's main concern is gettin' out to his deer lease and keepin' his wife happy. He's not doin' much in the way of investigatin'. Says it's the holidays."

"It's the holidays for the Vargas family, too," I pointed out.

"Well, his wife Lacey's been puttin' the screws to him lately. Says he's been workin' too much, is never home. But you and I both know that of all the crimes you could accuse Rooster Kocurek of committin', overwork ain't one of 'em."

"Too much time at the deer lease?"

"There's a competition to see who can get the biggest rack. Prize is one of those five-hundred-dollar coolers and braggin' rights for the year."

"So that's more important than a murder investigation and his wife? He'll be lucky if all he gets in his stocking is coal this Christmas," Molly said. "If I were Lacey, I might be tempted to stuff it with divorce papers."

"Well, she got pretty fed up with him last week," Opal said. "Said if he spent one more weekend at that deer lease, she was takin' the kids to her momma's house for Christmas. He's been online lookin' at diamond necklaces ever since."

Flora was knitting, her needles clacking and her stitches getting smaller and smaller. "Maybe I shouldn't go out on this date. Maybe I should stay single."

Opal's head swiveled. "You got a date, honey? With who?"

"Gus Holz," she said. "We're going to the Hitching Post for a drink after the Market."

Opal nodded. "Gus is a good man. A bit quiet, and maybe not a beauty queen contestant, if you know what I mean, but he's a good man. Plus," she said, winking, "he cooks. If I weren't married, I might think about askin' him out to drinks myself!"

Flora's shoulders dropped a little, so they were no longer around her ears, and the rate of clacking decreased. "Really?" she asked Opal.

"Really," Opal reassured her. "Besides, it's just a drink. If he gets too frisky, you just whack him over the head with your purse and go home."

She nodded. "I guess that makes sense. But... but what if he doesn't like me?"

"He asked you to drinks, didn't he?" Opal said. "He likes you. But honey, if you don't mind my sayin' so, you might want to tone down the lipstick."

Flora's hand leaped to her lips. "You think?"

Opal nodded. "I've got a real pretty pink you can try. I think it would make your lips look fuller. You can try it out before you go."

"Thank you," Flora said, looking at Opal as if she were some kind of dating goddess.

Opal turned toward me. "I heard you were helping out at Rosita's this morning. Is Mandy coming?"

I shook my head, pulled my stunted scarf from my knitting bag, and reached for a cookie. "She's got to get this week's issue out. I'm worried about her."

"Worried? Anything new?" Opal said.

I shrugged. "Her mom's sick and her sister's in jail.

Not exactly the ideal holiday season."

"Bless her heart," Opal said.

"Is Sheriff Kocurek making any progress on the investigation?" Flora asked.

"Far as he's concerned, it's an open-and-shut case," Opal said. "But Lucy here isn't convinced. For good reason; that Randy Stone wasn't the most popular man in Buttercup."

"What do you know about his sister Jenna?" I asked. "I heard she wasn't too happy about her brother being in line to inherit the business."

Opal narrowed her eyes. "You thinkin' she might be the one?"

I shrugged. "I'm just exploring all the possibilities right now. I wondered if you knew anything."

As I spoke, there was another knock at the door. Molly went to answer it; a moment later, Quinn came into the warm cozy kitchen, carrying her knitting bag on one shoulder, her cheeks flushed. "I can't stay long," she said, "but I wanted to check in."

"Lucy here was just asking about Jenna," Opal informed her as Molly gave her a mug of hot cider.

"What about her?" Quinn asked.

"I heard down at the Hitching Post that she wasn't too happy with her brother Randy."

"I'd heard that, too," Quinn said.

"What else did you hear?"

"Well, she was in the other day, talkin' on the phone," Quinn said, "and I heard her say she was afraid he would run the business into the ground if he had the chance."

"Might be worth mentioning to Rooster," I suggested to Opal.

"I'll tell him, but he won't listen."

"Did you mention Rhonda to him?"

"I did," she said, "but he figured she'd show up. Said if someone filed a missing persons report, he'd look in to it, but he hadn't heard anything."

I sighed. Rooster was many things. Helpful was definitely not one of them.

I headed home after adding about half an inch to Tobias's very short scarf, and spent some time catching up with things at the farm. I'd just finished harvesting some greens for the café and the Red and White Grocery when Tobias called.

"How do you feel about a trip to the Stone ranch this afternoon? " he asked.

I looked at the clock. I might be late to the Market, but it was a risk worth taking. "I'm in."

Chapter 7

THE STONE RANCH WAS ANYTHING but stony, as it turned out.

"This place is huge," I told Tobias as we bumped down the long winding road from the highway. Tobias had gotten a call about a lame cow, and I was along for the ride… and to see if I could sniff out any information.

Enormous Angus cattle browsed the pasture on either side of us, in clusters here and there on the hilly terrain. The land seemed well cared for; some overgrazed pastures seemed to consist of nothing but prickly pear cactus and mesquite trees, but even though it was winter, I could see that the vegetation wasn't picked completely clean, and that the land lacked the stressed look I often saw on poorly managed ranches.

"William Stone is a good rancher," Tobias confirmed. "He spends money to make sure his cattle are healthy; he's been moving into producing some grass-fed cattle, too."

"That means they don't go to the feedlot to get fattened up on grains, doesn't it?"

"Exactly. The meat is more expensive, but it's better for the animals—and the people who eat the meat."

Even though I was a meat eater myself, I still had a hard time with the idea of raising animals for food—

other than milk and eggs, that is. But if you were going to do it, I liked the idea of cows being able to enjoy a decent life outdoors. Not that outdoors in summer in Texas could be considered decent, but it sure was better than a feedlot.

"Have you met all the Stones?" I asked as the barns came into view. They were new, made of corrugated metal, and well maintained. The ranch house, a sprawling, stone building with two wings, was visible a short distance away, with a grove of oak trees sheltering it and a pond with a few geese floating placidly. Not a bad setup.

"I have," Tobias confirmed.

"What do you think of them?"

"I've only met them in passing. William Stone is a good stockman, though. He rotates his pastures and makes sure his animals are in good shape. I met Jenna a few times; she seemed to have a good head on her shoulders. She has a job in a bank in Houston somewhere, I think.

"And you've met Randy?"

"I have," he said. "Only once, though." He grimaced. "Frank was right, I think. All hat and no cattle. He was a good glad-hander, though."

"And more than that," I added, thinking of Rhonda, and her relationship with the now-deceased young man. "I guess he won't get the ranch now, at least. It's a lot of acreage."

"It is," Tobias agreed. "At least a thousand acres."

"Land's running around 12K an acre right now, isn't it? That's a lot of potential money in the bank."

"It's been in the family for fifty years. I don't know how much they owe on it, but unless they've refinanced, it can't be much compared to what it's worth."

He glanced at me. "Not a bad motive, is it?"

"It's not," I said. "Too bad we can't just ask who inherits."

"Not directly, anyway." Tobias pulled up next to one of the barns, and we both got out. There was the sound of a cow lowing from inside the building. When Tobias and I walked in, we were greeted by a young woman with blond hair scraped back into a ponytail and a pair of faded jeans with mud smears on the cuffs. She wore weathered boots and a flannel shirt that was two sizes too big for her, and her face was drawn.

"Dr. Brandt?" she asked in a pleasant, competent voice. She wiped her hands on the front of her jeans and offered one for him to shake.

"Good to see you, Jenna," Tobias said, taking her hand and shaking it. "This is my girlfriend, Lucy Resnick; she owns a small farm close to town. I'm so sorry about your brother," he added as they finished shaking hands and I proffered my own.

"Thanks," she said as she gave my hand a firm shake. "It's all been a shock. Mom went into the hospital yesterday, and my husband Simon and I've been helping Daddy out around the place while he stays with her. It's never a good time, but just before the holidays..." She grimaced. "It's been hard."

"I'm so sorry," I said, echoing Tobias. "Is there anything we can do to help?"

"Unless you can bring him back, I'm afraid not," she said. "Mother and Daddy are just beside themselves. I took off work until after New Year's, but I don't know what they're going to do when I have to go back to Houston."

"Don't you have help on the ranch? It's a big place to manage alone; I thought your dad had a few hands taking care of things."

"He does," she said, "but the place has to be managed. And Randy started a few projects I have to..." She trailed off. "It'll all work out," she said in a firm voice, then turned to the sick cow. "In the meantime, I'm hoping you can take a look at her back foot. It's swollen, and she's having a hard time walking."

"Hi, sweetheart!" There was a voice from the door to the barn. I turned to see a tall, good-looking man in designer jeans, a crisp white button-down shirt, and what appeared to be very expensive boots.

"Hi, Simon," Jenna said, brightening.

"What's going on out here?"

"Taking care of this cow," she said.

"Be careful," he said, putting a protective arm around her and kissing her on the top of her head. "I don't want anything to happen to you."

"You're sweet, " she said. "I'll be just fine. I've been doing this since I was a kid."

"You'd love it out here, wouldn't you?" he said. He turned to us. "What's it like, living in the country?"

"It's nice," I said. "Everyone knows everyone, and it's good to be away from the city."

"I guess we'll be spending more time out here, so I'll find out myself," he said.

"I'm sorry about your brother-in-law."

"Circle of life, I suppose," he said. "Randy and I were never close, but it's hard on Jenna and her family. Anyhow, I was just coming to check on my sweetheart. Nice to meet you," he said, and wandered out of the barn.

Jenna rolled her eyes. "I love him, but he's such a city boy."

I grinned. I was a city girl, too, but not quite in the

same way.

As Tobias tended to the lame cow, there was a lull in the conversation. I walked around the barn, which was in tip-top condition, then strolled outside.

The ranch house looked like it had been built in the fifties and added on to a few times, with a wing of similar stone with a slightly different color mortar and what looked like a second addition built from Hardie board. Someone was a gardener; the beds around the house were neatly maintained and mulched, with the shrubs cut back for winter, and a festive wreath decorated the door. A gaily painted wood Santa with a list of names had been placed lovingly in the front yard. I walked a little closer; it was Santa's "nice" list, and the names Chad, Randy, and Jenna had been hand-lettered at some point in the past. I knew about Randy and Jenna, but found myself wondering about Chad. Had the Stones had a third child? I made a mental note to ask Tobias.

As I walked toward the pond, I heard a thunk... but not from the direction of the house. It seemed to be coming from a building tucked into the trees behind the main house; it was a guesthouse, it looked like. As I watched, a woman with brown hair stepped out the front door and grabbed a pair of boots from the stoop before disappearing back inside. She didn't see me—at least I didn't think so—but I was pretty sure I recognized her.

Unless I was mistaken, it was Rhonda.

❦

I waited a few minutes to see if she'd come out again, but the little guesthouse stayed silent. I was still ostensibly watching the geese paddle around the pond, dipping their bills into the water from time to time, when Tobias called me from the barn.

"I think we're done here," he said as I ambled back to where he and Jenna were standing.

"Is she going to be okay?"

"I think so," he said. "Just a round of antibiotics and some time off her feet and she should be back in business."

"Great," I said. "This really is a nice place. Do you stay in the guesthouse when you're here?" I asked Jenna.

"Nobody's stayed in that guesthouse for years," she answered quickly, turning away from the house.

"I noticed three names on Santa's 'nice' list," I pressed, although I knew I probably shouldn't. "I recognized you and Randy, but I didn't know you had another brother."

"I don't," she said, her face turning flat and hard. "Now, if you don't mind, I have chores to do. Thank you for coming out, Dr. Brandt."

"My pleasure," he said. "I'll call and check in a day or two, to see how she's doing. And again, I'm so sorry about Randy. If there's anything I can do, let me know."

"I will," she said briskly. "Thanks." Her tone was dismissive, so we walked to the truck. We said nothing until Tobias had backed out of his spot and was well down the driveway.

I glanced into the side-view mirror. Jenna was watching us, as if making sure we weren't going to double back.

"What was all that about?" Tobias asked.

"I think I saw Rhonda," I told him. "In the guesthouse."

"Why would she be here?"

"That's what I was hoping Jenna would tell us," I replied. "But either she doesn't know Rhonda's there, or she's hiding her."

"Are you sure it was Rhonda?"

"Not a hundred percent, but it sure looked like her." I sighed. "I'm sorry I made things awkward. I just have a feeling Jenna knows more about things than she's letting on."

"You mean about what happened to Randy?"

"Maybe," I said.

"She's a good candidate for a suspect, I'll give you that. And she sure didn't want to talk about that third name on the Christmas decoration."

"Did the Stones lose a child?"

"I don't know," Tobias replied. "I never asked. I'll bet Opal would know, though... or the county clerk."

"I think I'm going to look in to it," I told him. "I have a feeling there are some dark secrets in the Stone family... and that they could be linked with what happened to Randy."

"Nothing like a murder to brighten up the holidays, eh?" Tobias asked as he turned onto the highway.

"And don't forget missing persons," I added.

"Although if Rhonda is staying in the Stones' guesthouse, maybe she's not missing after all."

"Why would she be there, anyway? If Jenna does know about her, why would she let her stay there?"

"I don't know," Tobias said. "You're right, though; I think there's more going on."

"What do you know about Jenna?"

"She's been married to Simon for a few years; he does real estate stuff in Houston," he said. "They don't have kids; she's pretty serious about her job, from what I've gathered."

"But she wants to be involved in the ranch."

"I think it's about protecting her inheritance," he said. "And her brother not drinking away the profits. It's a pretty tight ship under William. I'm not sure Randy had what it takes to keep that going, from what we've heard about him."

"I wish we had a competent sheriff," I said.

"Speaking of competence, Rooster's in the hospital," Tobias informed me.

"What?"

"He shot himself in the foot with a rifle. Literally."

I know it was wrong, but I laughed out loud. "Are you sure his wife didn't do it?"

"No," he said, "but she did file for divorce."

"It's never a dull moment in Buttercup, is it?"

He laughed. "Unfortunately not."

❧

Flora got to the Market well before I did. She was still wearing her bright red dress, but she had followed Opal's advice and toned down the lipstick.

"How can I help?" she asked as I lowered the tailgate on the truck. I hadn't had time to do as much prep work as I'd hoped; although I'd cut another batch of soap, I'd have to label them while we were tending the booth. I still had a good bit of mistletoe, though. Maybe I should give a sprig to Flora.

"If you'll just get everything set up, that would be great," I said. "I've got to get these labels on the soaps. I ran out of time today."

"Of course!" she said, darting a glance toward Gus's booth. I followed her gaze; Gus was staring back at her, a slightly goofy grin on his broad features. I almost asked her about her upcoming date, but before I could say anything, Molly hurried up to the stall. "Did you hear about Rooster?" she asked.

"Which part?" I replied.

"I guess you have heard, then."

"Is he going to be okay?"

"He's already out and on crutches," she told me. "But Lacey told him if he's so in love with his deer blind, he should stay there."

"Ouch," I said. "To both. Hey," I added in a quieter voice, "I know Alfie knows the Stones pretty well. What do you know about Jenna?"

"She's sharp," Molly acknowledged. "Her brother practically had to get a GED, but she was valedictorian. Got married a few years back and moved to Houston, but she comes home a lot." She paused. "I did hear something, though."

"What?"

"She and Simon weren't having luck having children. There was some talk of adoption not long ago, but I heard her daddy told her the ranch would only go to grandkids related by blood. I think they spent a bundle on IVF, but as far as I know, they haven't had any luck."

"That's hard," I said. I'd had friends in Houston who had experienced infertility. In a way, being unable to have a child was like a death in its own right. I'd never had a strong yen for offspring, but I sympathized with those who wanted children and couldn't have them.

"It just doesn't seem right," Molly said, echoing my thoughts, "that good people who want kids can't seem to get pregnant, and others end up with children they don't really want. You'd think God would do something about that, wouldn't you?"

"You'd think. Mysterious ways and all, I guess." But now I was thinking about the Stones. "Randy and Isabella didn't have kids, did they?"

"No," Molly said. "They'd only been married a year or so. Isabella wanted to wait, from what I hear. I gather things were a little shaky financially."

"I kind of got that impression, too," I replied.

"Any word on Rhonda?" Molly asked.

"No," I said. "But between you and me, I could have sworn I saw her at the guesthouse at the Stones' place today. Jenna told me there was no one staying there."

"Weird," Molly said. "Jenna and Rhonda were never really friends. Why would she be hiding her?"

"And why would Rhonda need to hide?"

"Maybe letting her husband cool down a bit?" Molly suggested.

"Maybe," I said, but I wasn't convinced. "I'll have to swing by the hair place where she works. Even if she's not there, maybe someone will have some idea where to find her."

As I spoke, the lights strung throughout the Market lit up, and "Happy Holidays" started playing on the PA system.

"I'd better go help the seventh-graders get ready for the concert," Molly said. The Buttercup Middle School Choir was scheduled to perform at eight.

"Tell Ethan to break a leg for me. And if you hear anything else, let me know."

"Don't I always?" Molly said with a grin.

It was only after she left that I realized I'd forgotten to ask about the third name on the sign in front of the Stones' house. Next time I saw her, I told myself as I picked up another label.

The next twenty minutes were pretty much eaten up

by soap labeling. By the time the first rush of shoppers appeared, eating candied almonds out of cones, sipping mulled wine or mead, and humming along to the Christmas carols wafting on the crisp December air, Flora and I had gotten the stall in decent shape.

"I just love this lavender soap," Flora said, taking a deep whiff of one of the creamy bars I had put out on display. "Have you thought about selling room sprays, or perfumes, or sachets? I'd love to put one of these in my lingerie drawer."

"I sold out of sachets, but the room spray is a good idea," I said. "I know Hill Country Lavender Farm sells oils, but I hadn't thought about a scented spray." It was definitely worth thinking about. A mix of lavender oil with grain alcohol or another carrier would make a great spritz for freshening rooms. I had some clove and orange oils back at the farm, too; I might experiment with a Christmas spray similar to the scents I used in my soaps.

"Maybe some bath oils, too," Flora suggested. "My skin always gets so dry in the winter."

"You're a natural marketer," I told her. "You'll have to come help me experiment sometime."

"Really?" she asked.

"Really," I said. "I've been thinking of putting up an online store for my soaps; it would be great to add some of these other products, too."

She took another whiff of the soap. "I'd love to help. I'm afraid I don't have very many good ideas, though."

"Are you kidding me, Flora? You just suggested a whole new product line!"

She beamed. "I'd love to help, Lucy."

"Let's get started after Christmas," I said. I'd put a lot of projects on hold—including my own future guesthouse, which needed serious renovation—until after the holidays. There would be a brief respite before calving and kidding started in February, and I hoped to get the website designed and a good bit of the guesthouse done. Ideally, I'd have it open and for rent in time for spring bluebonnet season, but I'd just have to take it as it came.

The Buttercup Middle School Choir knocked it out of the park with a medley of traditional carols mixed with fun modern holiday favorites like "Jingle Bell Rock," and the shoppers were in a spending mood. By the time the Market wrapped up, I had sold at least forty bars of soap, and most shoppers had expressed interest in the idea of a line of complementary bath products.

As the Market wound down, Flora was increasingly edgy, and I saw her cast more than one nervous glance across to Gus. When we closed up shop, I told her to go ahead. "I'll take care of it," I said. "There's not that much left to pack up anyway."

"Are you sure?"

"I'm sure," I said as she whipped out a cracked compact and reapplied the lipstick Opal had given her earlier. "Go relax and have fun," I advised her. "And one step at a time."

"Thanks, Lucy." No sooner had she spoken than Gus appeared, wearing what looked like his best button-down shirt and jeans that had been ironed into creases. Flora wasn't the only anxious one, I was guessing as I watched him run a meaty finger under his collar.

"I wrapped up a few minutes early," he told her, "so I'm ready to go whenever you are."

"Have fun!" I told them. Flora hesitated, then smiled

tentatively.

"Okay," she said, and I watched as they walked toward the Hitching Post together. When they started, you could have driven a tractor between them and not touched them. By the time they got to the corner, though, the distance had decreased to horse-width. I took it as a good sign.

Chapter 8

TOBIAS DROPPED BY THE STALL as I was loading the rest of my stock onto the back of my truck. "How'd you do?" he asked.

"Not too bad; I think I'll be able to pay the mortgage this month," I answered. "I've got tamales from Rosita's; want to come over and share them with me?"

"I'd love that," he said. "Need help packing up?"

"I've only got that box of soaps and I'm done," I said, pointing to the small wooden box on the table. As he picked it up, I noticed the mayor coming out of the courthouse door. I hadn't heard any more about the courthouse discovery... but I wanted to let her know what I'd seen the night before.

"Mayor Niederberger!" I called. She caught my eye and waved. "Can you keep an eye on the stall for me?" I asked Tobias. "I want to touch base with her."

"Happy to," he offered, and I hurried over to greet the mayor.

"How are things at the farm?" the mayor asked as I approached her.

"Fine for now," I said. "Of course, that could all change tomorrow, but I can't complain. Any more news on the bones, or on the paintings you found?"

"Nothing on the bones, but making progress on the paintings. An appraiser in Houston came out to look at them. I won't lie; they could be worth a bundle. Enough to pay for the renovations... but we'll have to decide if we keep them or sell them."

"Whose are they?"

"That's the question," she said. "Nobody knows. I've got the police seein' if they can figure out who might have stashed them. We're lookin' to see if there might be more hidden in the building somewhere, but so far we haven't found any. I'll show you where we found them, if you want to see."

"Sure," I said, following her to the door of the courthouse.

She pulled a key from her pocket and unlocked it, then opened the door and shone a flashlight inside the dusty, wrecked interior. On the outside, the courthouse was all white paint and Christmas lights, but the inside wasn't much more than a shell of weathered lumber and rotten floorboards. An electric drill and a few saws lay around, along with other construction—or, in this case, *destruction*—debris. A whiff of candied nuts eddied through the open door, but it wasn't enough to dispel the smell of age and must.

"Where were the paintings?" I asked as she flashed her light around.

"Someone walled them up over there," the mayor said, pointing to a square made of studs. "There was a loose panel, it looked like. Someone hid them; if they were going to come back for them, they never did."

"This place used to operate as a jail, didn't it?" I asked.

"It did," she said. "Folks say it's haunted, but I never saw anything. I think it's just because it's run-down and old." She pointed up to the framed ceiling. A few boards lay across it, and the remnants of a staircase squatted in the middle of the first floor. "The cells were up there.

You can still see some of the metal cages. It must have been miserable in the summer, with the heat."

"I'll bet," I said as the light glinted on a bit of metal. From what I could see, they looked like two oversize rabbit hutches. "They certainly must have been a disincentive to crime."

"You'd think," she said, "But there was a lot of cattle rustlin' back then. We had a few famous prisoners here in Buttercup."

"Who?"

"One was supposedly a train robber," she said. "He stayed in one of the cells for two days, but he escaped before he could go to trial."

"I didn't know we had a famous train robber in town," I said.

"Briefly," she said. "He was killed a week later in Dallas. Turned out he would have been better off staying put."

"That still doesn't explain the paintings, though, does it?"

"No," she said. "It's a mystery. I keep hoping the sheriff'll turn up something, but that's probably a pipe dream. We'll see what the appraiser says." She walked over to the back door and tried the knob; the door swung open. "I locked this last time I was here," she said. "What the heck?"

"Maybe it's the ghost of the train robber," I suggested jokingly. "Doesn't like being cooped up."

Together, we picked our way back to the front door. "You should come take a look at the paintings; I have them in my office for now, but we're going to have to figure out what to do with them."

"I guess if they're worth something, they'll need to be insured."

"We'll take that as it comes," she said. "In the mean-time, I've got other fish to fry. Like our sheriff. Wounded in the line of duty, he tried to tell me. Wounded in the act of drinking one too many Lone Stars in the deer blind, if you ask me. I feel bad for the man, but you can see why Lacey filed."

"I'm more worried about Isabella Stone," I said. "I've been asking around, and it sounds like Randy Stone had something of a reputation around town."

"I'd heard that, too," she said. "I might put a bug in Deputy Shames's ear, see if she might want to look in to that a bit more. Just between you and me," she added in a low voice, "our sheriff isn't the sharpest blade in the drawer on the best of days. And now, with Lacey filin' for divorce and him shootin' himself in the foot..."

"I understand," I told her. I was about to mention Rhonda to her, but something held me back. I was pretty sure Rhonda was currently bunking at the Stones' ranch. Besides, I wanted to go check out Shear Perfection before raising the alarm. If Rhonda didn't show up for work, I decided, I'd get in touch with the deputy.

"Stop on by whenever you like," the mayor offered again. "They're pretty paintings."

"Thanks," I said. "And thanks for talking to Deputy Shames."

"My pleasure," she said. "I just hope we get all this unpleasantness cleared up. Not the best way to go into the holiday season."

I wasn't sure it was possible to clear up the unpleas-antness—after all, Randy Stone was dead—but I knew I'd sleep better knowing the wrong person wasn't in jail for the crime.

"These are fabulous," Tobias said as he took his first bite of tamale at my kitchen table forty minutes later. After I'd finished packing up, he'd followed me back to my place, and together we'd steamed the tamales Mandy had given me.

"They are," I said. "She promised to give me the recipe, but I think I'd rather pick them up from Rosita's. They're pretty time-consuming, and I'm not what you'd call a gifted corn-husk wrapper."

"You have other gifts." Tobias paused to take another bite, then added, "And speaking of your other gifts, what's for dessert?"

"I thought I'd toss a pudding cake in the oven," I said. "It only takes a few minutes to whip up, and they're best warm."

"I'm happy to be your sous chef," he volunteered, and took another bite of tamale. "Another couple of years of eating like this, and I'm going to be a natural for Santa." He patted his flat stomach, and I rolled my eyes.

"I'll just put you to work doing chores," I reassured him. "That'll burn off any excess."

"No, thank you," he said. "I've got enough on my plate as it is." He speared another piece of tamale and dipped it in salsa. "All that talk of the courthouse got me thinking, by the way; where are you on renovations of the little house?" I'd shared what the mayor had told me while the tamales were steaming.

"I've got a few contractors lined up. The German Club made a donation to help, and I have a little bit of reserve left from those gold coins we found," I said, "but I'm not sure it'll be enough."

"Renting it out in the spring and fall should pay for it pretty quickly, though, don't you think?"

"That's the hope," I said. "Maybe you can go over the plans with me sometime." I'd sketched out what I wanted for the contractor a few weeks ago: a bathroom downstairs, under the stairs, a living area on the left side and a kitchen on the right, and the upstairs loft partitioned into two bedrooms. The estimate had been disturbingly high, and I was still trying to figure out where to cut back. When it was finished, the house wouldn't be huge, but it would be cozy. I was hoping we could restore the wood floors, but if they were too far gone, I'd slap a coat of paint on them.

"Are you keeping that blue stencil on the downstairs walls?"

"Of course," I said. "The big expenses are going to be the kitchen, the bathroom, and the HVAC system. And bracing the building so it doesn't collapse in the next tropical depression."

"Not to mention patching the holes in the roof," Tobias added.

I groaned. Right now, I had a variety of pots and pans scattered around to catch drips. I sometimes wondered if I'd made the right decision, letting myself get talked into moving the old homestead to the farm. This was one of them.

Tobias must have seen the dismay on my face; he reached out and touched my hand. "You don't have to do it all at once," he said. "And it doesn't have to be *House Beautiful*. There's charm in 'just enough.'"

"Thanks," I said. "I just hope 'just enough' isn't 'way over my budget.'"

"What is it they say about old houses and money?"

"Whatever it is, don't tell me. I own two of them.

And my water heater's going south, too."

"Maybe we should start on that pudding cake," he suggested. "And maybe a beer or two."

"I like how you think," I said as he got up and grabbed two Shiner Christmas ales out of the fridge. He took the tops off and handed one to me.

"Now," he said after I'd taken a swig. "Let's talk about more cheerful things."

"Like Randy Stone?" I suggested. "Or Rhonda Gehring?"

"You really think you saw her today, don't you?"

"I do," I told him. "I just can't figure out why Jenna would be harboring her."

"I hope she is," Tobias said. "I hate to think of anything happening to her."

"I'm going to the hair salon where she works tomorrow," I told him. "If she didn't show up for work, I'm going to file a missing persons report."

"Has anyone heard from her husband?"

"Keith? I didn't see him at the Market tonight. Opal told me she left a message for him, but she hasn't heard back. Which worries me."

"You think he might have done something to Rhonda?"

"I hope not," I said. And I hoped I was right about what I'd seen at the Stones' ranch that afternoon.

"I guess you'll know more tomorrow," he said. "Now, tell me more about this pudding cake of yours."

"Let me just finish this tamale, and I'll show you!"

❧

We had the cake in the oven fifteen minutes later. I nibbled on the remains of a tamale, savoring the spicy, hearty combination of masa and beef freshened by tomatillo salsa laced with fresh onion and cilantro, and then slipped Chuck a piece while Tobias wasn't looking. "Don't tell," I whispered to him, and petted him on the head. He rewarded me with a few licks, then went and stood by his food bowl. "Subtle," I told him.

"How's he doing on the Light and Lean?" Tobias asked as I opened the oven and checked on the cake.

"He doesn't love it," I confessed.

"But you're not giving him extra treats, right? Other than carrots?"

"Well, occasionally," I admitted. "He's not a big fan of carrots."

"Try celery, then. Or cucumber."

Chuck gave me a look that made me wonder how much he really understood, and I nodded and promised to up Chuck's vegetable consumption. Or try to.

At least I didn't give him any cake.

Tobias stayed until eleven, and I was half-hoping he might spend the night again, but he deferred. "I've got to check in on one of the cases at the clinic, and I've got a seven a.m. appointment," he told me as he kissed me good night. "We'll do it soon, though."

As I watched his truck head down the driveway, I wondered about things. I'd sensed some hesitation, some drawing back. Had we pushed things too fast? We still hadn't discussed our Christmas plans, either. My parents were going to Italy for Christmas, so I was planning on tucking in at home. Molly had invited me, but I'd been hoping to spend the time with Tobias; the topic hadn't come up yet.

I'd bring it up tomorrow, I decided. Why were relationships so challenging? I thought of Isabella and Rhonda and Keith and Randy Stone, and the tangled mess they had made. My thoughts turned to Flora, and her jitters over her first date. Had it gone well? I wondered. Or would her heart be broken a second time?

Life was full of challenges, I told myself as I turned and went back inside. And on the plus side, at least we weren't stabbing each other in the back with kitchen knives.

Chapter 9

SHEAR PERFECTION WAS A SMALL store in a strip mall not far from the H-E-B grocery store in La Grange. I walked past ads for Brazilian blowouts and highlights and opened the glass door, letting out the small of chemicals and floral shampoo. I scanned the eight chairs lining the walls. Three of them were occupied, but there was no sign of Rhonda.

The young man at the front desk smiled at me. "Can I help you?"

"I'm looking for Rhonda Gehring," I told him. "I was hoping she could fit me in."

"Rhonda's not working today," he said.

"Oh, that's too bad," I said. "The shop owner told me she'd be here today. Is she sick?"

"She requested some personal time, I believe," he said. "Is there someone else who can help you?"

"I was really hoping to have Rhonda take care of me," I said. "Any idea when she'll be back?"

"Let me get the manager," he said, and headed to the back.

As he disappeared, one of the stylists, a thirty-ish woman with vivid red hair that was most likely not the color she was born with, excused herself and walked over to me. "Just between you and me, I'm not sure she's coming back. I'd be happy to help you out."

"Thanks," I said. "What's your name?"

"Sadie," she told me.

"I'm Lucy," I told her. "Did you talk with Rhonda?"

She nodded. "Something's going on... she's leaving town for a while. Wanted to keep it quiet, but I don't know why."

"I'm actually worried whether she's okay," I confided. "Did she tell you where she was going?"

"No," she said. "Just that there was an opportunity she couldn't pass up. She wasn't allowed to tell me details, though."

That didn't sound good.

I looked up; the young man was emerging from the back with a woman in tow. I fished in my pocket for a card and gave it to her. "Please give me a call if you hear anything. I'm worried about her."

She looked at it. "Dewberry Farm? My boyfriend got some of your jam at the Buttercup market this summer; it was amazing!"

"Really?" Thanks!" As I spoke, the manager came up to me with a bright smile. "I hear you were looking for Rhonda?"

"I was," I said. "I was hoping she'd be able to clean up this mop," I said, tousling my hair. It was getting a bit overgrown.

"I've got an appointment free in ten minutes," Sadie offered.

"You know what? I'll take you up on that," I said. I could use a haircut... and I had a feeling Sadie might be able to help me out a bit more than she already had.

"I'll be with you in a few, then," she said with a smile.

I sat down in the little waiting area and browsed through magazines filled with impossibly perfect women, and recalled why I hadn't put in a TV at my house; I somehow felt better about myself when I wasn't surrounded by images of airbrushed models. I was looking at a *Real Simple* magazine, which was suggesting buying organizers to organize your excess stuff, when Sadie called me back.

"What are we doing today?" she asked, fluffing my hair when I sat in the chair.

"Just a trim, I guess," I said.

She made a small moue with her lips. "You've got some grays coming in here. You want to cover them?"

"Not this time," I said. "Just a trim."

"But you'd look so good with a bit of color," she said. "It would brighten you up."

"What kind of color are we talking about?"

"Just a few highlights to frame your face," she said. "I can do it half off," she said. "Try it; I think you'll love it."

I thought of those magazines, and Tobias's reluctance to stay over. His ex-girlfriend was beautiful, and always had highlighted hair and a manicure. The manicure wasn't going to work—I was a farmer now, not an office worker—but a little bit of pizzazz couldn't hurt, could it?

"Sure," I said with a bit of misgiving as I looked at her brilliant red hair. "But nothing too... drastic, okay?"

"Of course not!" she said. "Subtle. It'll brighten you up for the holidays," she promised, and before I had a chance to back out, she'd disappeared to the back to mix up her concoction.

While she was gone, the stylist at the chair next to mine finished with her client and drifted back to clean up her station. "I hear you're looking for Rhonda," she said quietly.

"I am," I said. "I'm concerned about her."

"I talked with her the other day. She was worried about her husband."

"What about him?"

"She was planning on leaving him," she said in a quiet voice. "She didn't know how he was going to take it. He had a bad temper. I offered for her to stay with me, but she told me she had options."

"Did she say what they were?"

"She told me she had a friend who was going to look after her for a while. That she needed to stay away from the chemicals here, anyway."

"Why?"

"She didn't say. She just said she was going to take a break. I had a bad feeling about it, though; she wouldn't tell me what was going on. It sounded kind of fishy."

"When did you last talk with her?"

"Two days ago," she said.

"Do you know how to get in touch with her?"

She shook her head. "I've texted and called, but no response."

I reached into my pocket and grabbed another business card, thankful I'd thought to snag a few before leaving the farm that morning. "If you hear anything, please let me know. I used to be a reporter for the *Houston Chronicle*. I think something's wrong, too."

Her eyes got big. "You think something bad's happened to her?"

"I don't know," I said truthfully. If I hadn't seen her—or thought I'd seen her—at the Stones' ranch, I would have said *yet*. "I'm trying to find out."

"I'm glad," she said. "Rhonda was nice, but she was all over the place. No self-control. It was like she was on a mission to destroy her life."

"What do you mean?"

"She was doing some crazy stuff. Ever since she started seeing that guy..." Her eyes got big. "Oh. I shouldn't have said that."

"I know about him," I said.

"I heard his wife killed him. Stabbed him in the back."

"To be honest, I'm not quite sure that's what happened."

Her eyes got even bigger, which I hadn't thought was possible. "You don't think Rhonda did it, do you?"

"I don't know what happened," I said. "That's what I'm trying to find out."

"We're all ready!" Sadie sang as she returned from the back room with two bowls and some brushes. Thirty minutes later, my head was covered in little strips of foil, and my "Why not?" insouciance had turned to something like terror.

"Twenty minutes, and we'll take it all out," she said.

"What's it going to look like?" I asked.

"You'll love it!" she said. Her phone beeped, and she looked at it. "I'll come get you when it's time," she said, and she left me stranded with a head that looked something like a modern-art sculpture.

I walked out of Shear Perfection about an hour later without any additional information that might lead me to Randy Stone's killer, but with a bag filled with expensive hair-care products I really couldn't afford and a head of hair that looked a little out of place combined with my flannel shirt and jeans.

When Sadie first showed me my new look in the mirror, I hadn't known what to say.

"Do you like it?" she'd asked as I stared at my hair, which had been transformed into a streaky burnished gold mane.

"Wow," I'd said. "It's beautiful," I told her truthfully, "but it doesn't feel like me."

Her shoulders sagged. "You don't like it?"

"No," I told her. "It's not that." I turned and looked at myself in the mirror. The color complemented my eyes and did make my face seem brighter somehow, and the cut framed my face beautifully. "I love it," I told her honestly. "I just don't know if I can keep it looking like this."

"It's easy," she said, and launched into a long description of products and hair-drying techniques that flew right over my head. I didn't have the heart to tell her I didn't own a hairdryer, but I did end up buying the "smoothing" shampoo and conditioner. It was more than I wanted to spend, but I figured I'd wrap it up and give it to myself as a Christmas gift.

Which reminded me, I thought as I left the salon: I still didn't have a tree. Tobias and I had talked about going out to cut one at a Christmas tree farm, but we were running out of time. I'd stop by the Red and White Grocery on the way home, I decided, and pick up one of the small trees I'd seen on the sidewalk.

And maybe some gossip, too.

"Wow!" Edna Orzak said when I walked through the door of the little grocery store a short time later. "What did you do to yourself?"

"I didn't do anything," I said, blushing. "I got a haircut in La Grange."

"More than a haircut," she said. "I love that color on you."

"Thanks," I told her.

"Where'd you get it done?" she asked.

"Shear Perfection," I told her.

"Did Rhonda do it for you?"

"You know Rhonda?"

"Of course!" Edna said. "She used to come in here all the time when she was a girl. She always got strawberry Twizzlers. Her mama had to call and tell me not to sell her more than one pack a day. Said she wasn't eatin' her supper."

"Have you talked with her the last few days?"

She shook her head. "No," she said. "Last time I saw her, she was buying a big ol' bottle of Pepto-Bismol and a half gallon of Blue Bell Peppermint Ice Cream." She glanced over at the freezer. "I don't know what they put in it, but that stuff is like a drug. I put a scoop of it in some hot chocolate the other day, and let me tell you, that's some good stuff. Speakin' of good stuff, Flora tells me you're thinkin' of expanding your line of products."

"When did you see Flora?" I asked. I'd totally forgotten about her date.

"Just this mornin'," Edna said. "She was walkin' on air."

"Was she?"

"Well, she and Gus closed down the Hitchin' Post last night, from what Frank told me. Sounds like a little holiday romance. Won't be surprised if Flora starts hangin' mistletoe all over town. Although based on what Frank told me, she won't need it; Gus is smitten." She shook her head. "All kinds of romantic stuff goin' on. Rooster's wife filin' for divorce—not that I blame her—Isabella killin' her husband..."

"I'm not so sure she did," I said.

"Well, I hear he was steppin' out on her."

"With whom?" I asked, wondering if the rumor mill had produced another potential suspect.

She pulled a face. "Margaret Rauch came in the other day to buy molasses for gingerbread, and she told me she saw Randy and Rhonda parked down on Ska-litsky Lane, but I don't know that I believe it. She's got a tongue like a snake."

So somehow, the news of Randy and Rhonda's affair hadn't broken wide open. I was surprised. "I heard he had a bit of mistletoe in his hair," I said. "Where do you think that might have come from?"

"Your stall at the Market, could be. I don't know," she said. "I haven't been lookin' for it. Now," she said. "I've been runnin' on here, and haven't asked what I can help you with."

"I'd like a Christmas tree," I told her. "We were going to go out and cut one, but I'm almost out of time."

"Lucky you," she said. "We just marked them down fifty percent this mornin'."

"How much for a small tree?"

"I can do you a five-footer for twenty-five dollars," she said. "I've got a few tiny trees left, but they're not really proper trees, are they?"

"Five feet sounds about right," I said, thinking of the corner of the cozy living room at the farm. I opened my wallet and pulled out some cash.

"Need anythin' else?" she asked. "We've got two half gallons of that peppermint ice cream left, if you're interested."

"I'll take one," I said.

"Good thinkin'," she said. "Folks are startin' to get

ready for the big holiday; I can't keep things in stock."
As she spoke, a young woman with a grocery cart piled
high with flour, brown sugar, baking chocolate, and
condensed milk pulled up to the register.

"What are you making?" I asked her as Edna counted
out my change.

"Fudge," she told me. "If you add in a couple drops
of peppermint extract and mix in some crushed candy
cane, it's amazing. I was going to send out recipes with
my Christmas cards; I've got one here if you'd like."

"I'd love one," I said as she fished in her purse and
pulled out a gaily printed index card. "Thanks so
much," I told her. "I'm Lucy Resnick, by the way."

"Tracy Keene," she said.

"She lives over by the Stone ranch," Edna informed
me.

"Oh? I was just out there yesterday with Dr. Brandt,
checking on a wounded cow. They've had a rough go
of it lately."

"They have," Tracy said. "Jenna is there all the time
now, trying to keep everything together." She shook
her head. "She always had the business sense, but her
daddy always had it in his head that Randy was the
one to take over the place." She grimaced. "I guess he
won't, now."

"How long have you known the Stones?" I asked.

"I grew up with them," she said. "We all went to
high school together. When we were just kids we used
to play down by the creek in the spring and fall. When
it wasn't all dried up, that is."

"I noticed a Christmas decoration on their lawn yesterday. There was kind of a Santa's list on it... only there
were three names on it, not two. Randy, Jenna, and
someone named Chad."

She grimaced. "Chad was Randy and Jenna's big brother. He was about ten years older than us. When we were in middle school, he got into some huge fight with his dad and just took off."

"Where did he go?"

She shrugged. "Nobody knows. He just up and disappeared. Let me see... Randy was a senior in high school then. Jenna and I must have been just about to start middle school."

"And he never came back?"

Tracy shook her head. "They never saw him again—leastwise, if they did, they never talked about it. Me," she said, "I would never let one of mine disappear without searchin' the rest of my life, but everyone's different, I suppose."

"A lot of tragedy in that family."

"Too much," she said, glancing at her watch. I realized the line had grown a bit while Tracy and I were talking.

"I'd better go get that tree," I said. "Thanks for the chat—and for the recipe."

"My pleasure," she said. "Hope you have yourself a good holiday."

"Likewise," I said. "If you're at the Market, stop by and see me!"

"Will do!" she said as Edna started to scan her groceries.

I stepped outside into the brisk December air, my heart hurting for the Stone family. I couldn't imagine what that must be like. I didn't have children of my own, but I knew it would be absolutely heartbreaking.

The tree selection wasn't huge, but there were some good options, and none of them were losing their needles. I picked a pretty fir tree, and had grasped the trunk and was carrying it to the truck when I heard what I'd swear was Jenna Stone's voice, coming from around the corner. I put down the tree and walked over to the corner of the Red and White Grocery, pretending to be inspecting the balsam wreaths Edna had hung up for sale, and stole a glance around the side of the store.

It was Jenna; her back was to me, and she was hunched up with a cell phone to her ear.

"It'll work," she was saying. "I promise you. It's just another six months, and it'll all be over."

Chapter 10

I COULD HEAR A MAN'S VOICE on the other end of the phone.

"Do you have any other suggestions?" she asked tartly. "Because I'm all ears."

Another volley of words I couldn't hear. Whoever was on the other end of the line seemed very upset.

"Unless you've got an alternative, this is the plan. Now, I've got errands to do. I'll call you later."

She jabbed at the phone with an index finger. As I slid back out of sight, I heard someone call my name.

"Lucy!"

I turned to see Flora hurrying across the Square toward me. She was wearing a bright green velour turtleneck dress with a wide belt and knee-high boots, and giant, flashing Christmas light bulbs dangled from her ears. And it looked like I hadn't been the only one to go to the hair salon, either; her formerly rather dull brown hair was now the color of carrot cake. It actually kind of suited her.

I glanced toward where I'd been standing a moment ago, just as Jenna emerged from the side of the building. Our eyes met for an instant. Unless it was my imagination, she looked spooked. I smiled and gave her a half wave; she gave me a tight nod and turned back to disappear the way she'd come. Was she looking to see if

I'd been in range to hear her conversation?

I didn't have much more time to think about it, though, because Flora was upon me, smelling like a perfume counter.

"You look good as a redhead," I told her as I sniffed a balsam wreath, hoping to clear the air a bit.

"Thanks," she said. "I like your hair, too. I never thought you were the type to get highlights!"

"Me neither," I confessed, reaching up to touch my hair a bit self-consciously. Would Tobias like it? Would it seem like I was trying too hard? Nonsense, I told myself. There was nothing wrong with changing things up a bit from time to time. "So... how did your date go?"

"Oh, it was wonderful," she gushed. "He's just so wonderful. I think I'm in love."

"After one drink?" I asked. "That's a good sign, but you might want to slow down a bit."

"What do you mean?" she asked, looking confused. "First you say to give it a shot, and now you want me not to?"

"No," I said. "That's not it at all. Just... take it slow," I advised. "You haven't known each other that long. It takes time."

She bit her pink-frosted lip. "We're supposed to go back to the Hitching Post tonight after the Market. Do you think I should cancel?'

"No," I said. "Just maybe take a day or two off after tonight."

"You think?"

"Maybe," I said. "Talk to Opal, too. Maybe I'm just being overly cautious."

"Maybe," she repeated, looking droopy. Then she brightened. "Oh! Did you hear about the paintings?"

"No," I said. "What about them?"

"They came from a museum robbery about fifteen years ago. It was an exhibition in Dallas. The appraiser figured out who they belonged to."

"Really? How did they end up here?"

"That's the big question," Flora said. "Some folks say it's mixed up with that body they found under the courthouse. I don't know, though."

"I can't see how they would be connected," I admitted. "Is the town going to give the paintings back, then?"

"I don't see as they have a choice," Flora said. "It'd be nice if the museum pitched in a few bucks to help us finish the renovation, though. I gave a bit myself, but not near enough for all the work they're plannin' on."

"That was really good of you, Flora," I said.

She tucked her chin a little and blushed. "Thanks," she said. "It was the least I could do, after my mother and all that hullabaloo about the statue of her so-called great-great-grandfather."

"Where did that end up, anyway?"

"I think it's in a storage shed, to be honest. Once Mama was gone, there wasn't anyone to champion it, and, well, with that nose..."

The nose had rather resembled an oversize pickle. "Maybe it's better in the storage shed, after all," I said. It certainly was better than in the middle of the town green, which was where Flora's mother, Nettie, had wanted it. "How are you doing, running everything by yourself these days?"

"It's getting easier," she said. "Still, it would be nice to have company." Her face suddenly tensed up. "You don't think Gus is after me for my money, do you?"

"I don't know him," I confessed, "but Opal seems to

think he's a good man. And from what I saw the other night, he lights up when he sees you."

"Does he?"

"He does," I said.

"There's mistletoe hanging by the door of the Hitching Post," she said. "I keep hoping he'll stop me."

"There was mistletoe in Randy Stone's hair, too," I remembered. "Do you think it might have come from there?"

"I'd think it was from Rosita's."

"But there wasn't any mistletoe at Rosita's, at least not that I saw," I pointed out.

"Well, then, where'd it come from?"

"I don't know," I said. "It might be worth trying to find out. At any rate, I'd probably better get this tree home and get ready for the Market." I walked back to the tree I'd abandoned and gripped the trunk. I hadn't talked with Mandy in a day or two, I realized. It might be a good idea to check in to see if she or her sister had any more ideas about what might have happened to Randy.

"I'll be there if you want me," Flora said. "And here... let me help you with that."

"Of course I want you," I said as we laid the tree in the truck bed. "See you in a few!"

"I'll be there with bells on!" she replied.

If the Christmas light earrings were any indication, there was a good chance she wasn't joking.

The tree looked beautiful in the corner of the living room, and its fresh, piney scent suffused the small farmhouse. I'd whipped up a batch of apple muffins when I got home, and the mixed aroma of Christmas tree, cinnamon, apple, and woodsmoke in the air was intoxicating. I took a sip of my tea and surveyed my home with satisfaction. Everything in the rest of Buttercup might be going to heck in a handbasket, but at Dewberry Farm, it was cozy and warm and beautiful. I caught a glimpse of myself reflected in a window, and for the tenth time that afternoon, my hand jumped to my hair, touching the unfamiliar silky locks. I liked how it looked, although I wasn't sure what it would look like after a normal wash and wear. Would Tobias?

I pushed the thought out of my mind and focused on the cozy living room, with the slipcovered couch and bright red cushions, the mullioned windows framing the view of the rolling Texas countryside, the rag rug on the worn wooden floorboards and the Christmas carols playing on the radio. A fire was crackling in the woodstove, and as a cold wind whipped around the house, I hugged myself, glad to be safe and warm inside. The only potential problem was Chuck, who was sniffing the trunk of the tree in a suspicious way. I warned him not to do any "decorating" of his own and was attempting to lure him to the kitchen when my phone rang.

I grabbed my phone out of my pocket, shooed my poodle away from the tree, and looked at the Caller ID. It was Mandy Vargas. I picked up.

"What's up?" I asked as I lured Chuck to the kitchen.

"I was about to ask you the same thing," Mandy said. "Find anything out?"

"I'm chasing down a few potential leads," I told her, "but nothing concrete. How about you?"

"Nothing, really," she said. "Isabella's too upset to think straight, and between all the hullabaloo about the courthouse and my parents, I haven't had the time to look in to things like I wanted to."

"And Isabella has no idea who else might have wanted to kill her husband?"

"Not that she's told me," Mandy said. "I asked if she'd be okay if you dropped by; both she and Opal okayed it."

I glanced at my watch. "I've got some work to do before the Market, but I might just do that."

"You won't have to worry about Rooster, at least," she said. "He skedaddled for his deer lease. Says he's working 'off-site.' From what I hear, he's drowning his sorrows."

"You think Lacey will go through with it?"

"Wouldn't you?" she asked. "The real question is, what possessed her to marry him in the first place?"

I sighed. "Oh... one more thing. I know Randy had mistletoe in his hair. There wasn't any at Rosita's; is there any mistletoe at your place?"

"Nope," she said. "Romance isn't exactly on this year's wish list for me," she added somewhat bitterly.

"Well, keep an eye out," I said. "It could be key. Oh—you heard about the museum robbery, right?"

"I did," she said. "I'm doing a basic article on it for the next issue. Once I get this stuff with Isabella sorted out, I'll go into it in more detail."

"Still no word on the bones at the courthouse?"

"Nothing yet," she said. "Except that they haven't been there that long. So no ancient Indian burial ground, at least."

"This town is just full of mysteries, isn't it?"

"Too many, if you ask me," she said.

❧

I filled the back of the truck with what I needed for that night's Market. The soap had sold much faster than anticipated; next year, I'd have to make more. I might have to find other places to cut mistletoe, too, or invest in an extension ladder; my oak trees were looking a little bare this season.

I checked on all the girls, making sure they were fed and watered—the chickens were tucked up in the coop, sheltering from the wind, but the cows and goats were out inspecting the perimeter, as usual. Nobody had made a break for it in months; I hoped that meant we had all potential points of egress nailed down, but with Blossom and Hot Lips, you never knew. Even now, Hot Lips was testing the wire fence. I petted everyone and gave them each a carrot—Chuck might not like them, but they were a big hit with the livestock—and then headed to my truck, and to town.

Opal was working hard on her knitting project when I got to the sheriff's office.

"Well, I was wondering when I'd see you here," she said, brightening at the sight of the Tupperware container in my hand. "Is that for me?"

"Yes, but I was hoping you might share with Isabella," I said, handing her the container of muffins. "Is she here?"

"Where else would she be?" Opal asked dryly.

"Good point," I said. "Dumb question, really. Can I see her?"

"I'll ask," she said. "But seein' as she's rereading those *Texas Monthlys* for the third time, I can't imagine she'll say no.

She set down her knitting and headed to the back. I could hear voices, and then Opal returned, giving me a nod. "Let me put two of these on a plate for her, though," she said, opening the cabinet above the coffeemaker and retrieving a paper plate with an illustration of Rudolph. She laid two of the warm muffins on the paper plate, added a festive red napkin, and handed it to me. "I'll watch your purse," she said, and then led me back to Isabella.

"She brought you some warm muffins," Opal volunteered as I greeted Isabella. I'd met her a few times; she looked a little like her sister, Mandy, only wirier, with big, anxious-looking eyes. Her dark hair was pulled back into a messy ponytail, and she wore loose jeans and a faded blue sweater; evidently, they'd let her keep her own clothes.

"I'm not sure I can eat," she said, "but thank you."

"You need to eat," Opal said. "Keep your strength up."

Isabella sighed. "I'll try."

I set the muffins down on the little table by the bed, next to the stack of well-thumbed magazines, as Opal withdrew. There was a chair across from the bed; I sat there as Isabella retreated to the bed, wringing her hands.

"First," I said, "I'm so sorry for your loss."

She snorted. "I'm supposed to say 'thank you.' I know it looks bad if I don't say 'thank you.' But I never should have married that man. He brought nothing but pain and strife to me." As she spoke, tears began leaking from her eyes. "But I still miss him," she said. "Isn't that ridiculous? After all he put me through? I don't know what to think or feel anymore." Isabella swiped at her eyes with the back of her hand. "Sorry."

"No need to be sorry," I said gently, automatically reaching for a tissue and then realizing I didn't have my purse with me. "You've had a rough time lately."

"You can say that again," she told me. "I find out he's sleeping with that woman, and then he turns up with a knife in him." She waved at the little room. "And here I am."

"Life can change fast," I said. "It's a lot to take in. I'm hoping to help you, though; Mandy told you I used to be an investigative reporter. The Buttercup sheriff's office isn't exactly... well, it's not always the most proactive organization," I continued. "I told your sister I'd do what I can to find out what happened to your husband."

She looked up at me, and for a moment, she resembled a little girl. "You will?" she asked in a small voice.

"I will," I said. "But first, you've got to tell me where you went the night Randy died."

Her eyes flicked away, and she studied her ragged fingernails. "I didn't go anywhere."

"You did," I said. "Your tire tracks were in the driveway. If you didn't kill Randy, you shouldn't have anything to worry about."

"But I do," she said, and a kernel of misgiving hardened in my stomach.

Chapter 11

"WHY?" I ASKED QUIETLY.

She looked up at me. "Because I went back to Rosita's that night," she said in a quiet voice.

I said nothing, waiting for her to continue.

"I didn't want to," she said. "But Randy had... well, he had a problem with money. He drank too much, spent too much. I realized I hadn't emptied the cashbox that night... with all the tamale-making, it slipped my mind. If I didn't get it, I was afraid Randy would spend it all."

"So you went back to get the cash box," I prompted, thinking of what Julie had told me about what she saw the night Randy died. "What time was that?"

"I don't know. Maybe twelve-thirty?" she said. "I was upset; I know it was after midnight, though. When Randy didn't come home, I figured he was out on one of his sprees."

"Was the cash still there when you got to the restaurant?"

She nodded. "It was," she said, and then fell silent, studying her fingernails again.

"Did you run into anyone while you were there?" I asked.

"No," she said, too fast.

"Not Randy?"

She took a deep breath, then looked up at me. "Not in Rosita's, no," she confessed. "But he was in the parking lot. I'd already locked up, and was headed back to the car."

Well, that much lined up with what Julie had told me. "What did you do when you saw him?"

"He was angry," she said. "He wanted the money. I told him no, and got into my truck."

"Did he try to stop you?"

"No," she said. "He was never violent, I'll give him that. Like I said, I got back into the truck and came home and cried and cried until I fell asleep."

"Where did you put the cash?" I asked.

"In a shoebox in the back of my closet," she said. "I have to hide money from him. If he finds it, he spends it. When we bought the house, we had tons of equity, but he took out a second mortgage without telling me. Now, we've got nothing, and we can't afford the payments." She sniffled. "He was going to work for his dad, and that was supposed to help cover the payments, but now..."

"Did he have life insurance?"

"A little," she said. "Probably not enough, though. It's probably a good thing we weren't able to have kids," she said bitterly. "No father, and me in jail..." She burst into tears, burying her face in her hands. I moved over to sit beside her on the bed and put an arm around her. Her thin frame shook as I embraced her, and it was some time before the sobs subsided. "I'm so sorry," she said, her voice hoarse.

"No need to be sorry," I reassured her. "You're in a really bad situation. It's okay to be upset."

"But what do I do?" she asked. "I don't know who killed him. And I went to the restaurant the night he died. I lied about that."

"Randy had a key to the restaurant, didn't he?"

She nodded. "He was helping with the tamales, so he had an extra key made. When I figured out cash was disappearing, I was pretty sure it was him, but what was I going to say?"

"That is a tough one," I admitted. "Now, I have a hard, hard question to ask, but I have to ask it."

She swiped at her eyes. "It's about that woman he was seeing, isn't it?"

I nodded. "When did you find out?"

"I suspected," she said. "But I only found out when Keith Gehring told me, the night Randy died."

Not good. "Did you know Rhonda?"

She grimaced. "Only in passing. I knew she was an old girlfriend, but that was it. Although obviously we had a lot more in common than we knew."

"She's missing, you know," I said.

Isabella looked up at me. "What happened?"

"She and her husband aren't getting along," I said. "She's vanished."

"Do you think Keith had something to do with her disappearance?"

Since I was pretty sure I'd seen her at the Stones' house, and she'd called Shear Perfection since her disappearance, I doubted it, but I kept my thoughts on that to myself. "I don't know," I said. "How long had she and Randy been seeing each other? Do you have any idea?"

"Months, I think. At least. I really don't know. He only told me what he had to. If it weren't for those texts..." She teared up again. "How could I have been so blind?"

"It's not your fault," I told her, giving her another

one-armed squeeze. "Please don't blame yourself."

"It's hard," she said. "What's wrong with me? Why didn't he love me?" She dissolved into tears again.

"I'm so sorry, Isabella," I said. It must be horrible, being locked up here days before Christmas with nothing to think about but the loss of her husband—and his infidelity. "I feel confident, though, that what happened had everything to do with him and nothing to do with you."

"I wish I could believe you," she said, sniffling. She reached for a tissue from a box at the end of the bed and blew her nose loudly.

"In the meantime, though," I said once she'd wiped her nose and gotten herself somewhat back together, "I need your help figuring out who else might have wanted Randy dead."

She took a deep breath and moved away a little bit, so I dropped my arm, which had still been encircling her shoulders. "Okay," she said. "Think, Isabella. Who else?" After a moment, she came up with the obvious suspect. "Rhonda's husband Keith could have done it," she said. "I imagine he was as upset as I was."

"From what I understand, he was pretty angry," I said. "I haven't talked with him, but do you know if he was friends with anyone who might be willing to talk to me?"

She shook her head. "I don't really know him."

"Me neither," I said. "I'll keep asking around. Anyone else? Maybe someone Randy was in business with?"

"I know things were going south with his business in Katy," she said, bitterly. "That's why he had to come up here all the time. Or at least that's what he told me."

"What was going on in Katy?"

"He was a salesman," she said. "Only he spent more

time out golfing than selling. His expenses were huge, but he wasn't making any sales." She sniffled. "He kept saying the big account was just about to come, but you know how it is..."

"It never did."

"Right. He got fired two weeks ago."

"Just in time for Christmas," I pointed out.

"We were about to lose the house," she said. "I found out he hadn't made the payments in three months. He was trying to get me to ask my parents for money, but with my mother's health problems..." She trailed off and dabbed at her eyes with a fresh tissue. "I told him he needed to talk to his parents. My parents gave us the down payment for the house. I work as the office manager for a medical office, but it's not enough to pay the mortgage." She sniffed. "I got time off to take care of my parents, but I haven't told them about this yet. If I ever get out of here, I probably won't have a job." Her face crumpled again.

"Let's take one thing at a time," I said softly, rubbing her shoulders. When she'd gotten herself somewhat back together, I asked, "Was there anyone from his work who might have held a grudge?"

She shook her head. "His boss. But he fired him. What else could he do?"

"What about Randy's family?" I prompted, wondering what Isabella's take on Stone family dynamics would be.

"His sister had no time for him," she said. "I never understood why at first—he always said she was just selfish—but now I get it. I was just too stupid to believe her before."

"Not stupid," I said. "Love does crazy things to us sometimes."

"Yeah," she said bitterly.

"Did he ever talk about his missing brother?" I asked.

She looked up. "How did you know about Chad?"

"I was over there with Dr. Brandt," I said, "and I saw the name on the Santa Claus on the front lawn. His name was still on the little list in his hand."

Isabella nodded. "Randy's dad wrote him off, but his mom, Linda... she was still totally broken up about him."

"Did they ever find out what happened to him?"

She shook her head. "His mom always said he'd had a hard time finding his way in the world, but he'd just gotten some big break—something in Houston or Dallas, I think. He fought with his dad about it and then took off. He headed up there, called to say he was okay, and then... nothing." She sniffled. "She told me she hired a private investigator to find out what happened to him, but he couldn't find anything. He tracked down the hotel room he was staying in, but he just... vanished. No wallet, no keys, nothing. He didn't check out, but he didn't leave anything in the room. The trail went cold after that."

"She didn't have any information about what kind of job it was?"

She shook her head. "No. He said he was just on probation, and he didn't want to jinx anything; he'd tell her more if he got hired long-term."

"Sounds shady."

"I thought so, too," she said. "It was a long time ago. She checks the mail every day, hoping he'll send a letter... She even got on Facebook to try to find him. I don't know if he changed his name or what, but no luck."

"Did he get along with his parents?" I asked, wondering if maybe his departure had something to do with a family feud.

"Randy always said Chad was his momma's favorite," she said. "I don't know how true that was, or if it was just because she missed him so much when he disappeared. He never said anything about how his daddy felt, and as long as I knew him, William never mentioned his name."

"Bad blood, do you think?"

"Maybe," she said. "I got the impression William was disappointed he didn't take to ranching. He was hoping to pass on the family business." She sniffled. "Randy was supposed to take over at some point. Truth is, though, we weren't having much luck in the kid department, so who knows? He felt strongly about keeping it in the family. We'd been tryin' for a year, but no luck. Although that's a blessing, now, I suppose." The huge tear rolling down her cheek belied that, but I didn't push it.

"You really have had a terrible year, haven't you?"

She nodded. "And now Mama's in the hospital, and I'm here..." She sighed. "I was hoping next year would be when things turned around, but..."

"You never know," I said with an optimism I didn't quite feel.

Chapter 12

"YOU GOING TO THE KNITTING group this afternoon?" Opal asked as I headed out from the jail.

"I'm going to try," I said, "but I still have a lot to do back at the farm before the Market tonight."

"I understand," she said. "I made almond crescents."

"Those amazing sugar-dusted cookies you made last year?"

She nodded. "The very same. I hope you can make it; if not, I'll save a few for you." She frowned a bit. "I hope the powdered sugar doesn't make my knitting sticky."

"Just have wet wipes around," I suggested. "Besides, things can be washed."

"They're already made anyway, so it's a little late to shift gears. Four o'clock? And I really do like your hair."

"Thanks," I said. "I'll do my best to make it!"

As I stepped out of the sheriff's office, trying to do a mental inventory of the afternoon's chores, the mayor waved me down.

"Any progress on the Stone case?" she asked.

"I'm working on it," I told her.

"Have a minute to look at those paintings?"

"I can spare a few," I said, thinking the odds of making it to the knitting group just kept getting slimmer.

"Come on down to my office," she said, waving me toward the small building that housed Buttercup's main political operation. I followed her, waiting while she sorted through a heavy ring of keys until she found the right one.

"Here we go," she said as she opened the door and stepped inside.

Mayor Niederberger was a practical person, and her office felt right in keeping with that aspect of her personality. Although the little house was quaint, everything inside it was no-nonsense, from the massive 1950s' era metal desk to the inexpensive metal filing cabinets that lined the wainscoted walls. The only nod to decor was a purple African violet blooming on the corner of her desk next to the window.

"Here they are," she said, opening a closet door and pulling out the paintings.

They were large oil paintings in a Renaissance style, featuring Mary and baby Jesus and what I was guessing were a couple of saints. I was raised Protestant, so I never learned to tell the saints apart, but it was obvious the paintings were done by a master.

"They're beautiful," I said, admiring the deep blue of Mary's dress and the gold-leaf halo around the baby's chubby head. "I can't believe they look so good after being shut up in the courthouse for so long. Heat, humidity, cold..."

"That's the thing," the mayor said. "We don't know how long they've been there."

"When were they stolen?"

"Thirteen, fourteen years ago," she told me. "It was a traveling exhibition; someone broke into the museum. The police showed up, but by the time they got there, these paintings were missing."

"Anything else?"

She shook her head. "Not that I know of, or that the museum knows of. They're happy to have them back, but I'm a bit disappointed. The renovation is costing me an arm and a leg. These old houses always do," she said, grimacing at the ceiling. "Just put a new roof on this place five years ago, and already it's leaking."

Well, that was encouraging, I thought, thinking of the little house on the knoll at Dewberry Farm I'd taken on. I hoped, for about the three-thousandth time, that I hadn't made a mistake.

"How are you getting them back to the museum?"

"They're comin' to pick 'em up this week," she said. "I figured out what happened, though."

"What do you mean?"

"How they ended up hidden," she said.

"Tell me?"

"Last time they renovated the courthouse was right around the time these paintings went missing. They were closing in a closet that was too shallow to really be a closet, reclaiming some of the space for another room. These were hidden behind a loose panel."

"A closet? I didn't know they had closets back then." My house certainly didn't.

"Well, maybe a storage room or somethin'," she said. "At any rate, when they opened it up, these were shoved in between the studs. Looks like someone walled them up to keep 'em safe, and was plannin' to come back and find 'em later."

"Why didn't they?" I asked.

"Good question," she answered. "And it still doesn't explain why there are bones under the floorboards."

"Is that where they were?"

"They were in the dirt," she said. "It was a shallow

grave right under the courthouse. Although why anyone would want to bury someone in a courthouse is
beyond me."

"Maybe because it was under renovation, it was convenient," I said. "If the murder was committed in the
courthouse, it would be an easy way to hide a body."

"Maybe," she said, sounding unconvinced. "All I
know is, some days I think we should just tear the
whole dadgum thing down and start over. There's
always some kind of trouble involving the courthouse
and the green."

"On the plus side, you won the statue debate."

She shivered. "Thank heaven for that," she said. "If I
had to look at that sausage nose every time I walked
to work, I might consider runnin' for office in La
Grange." She fell silent, and together our eyes drifted
to the paintings. They were like a window into a different time, and I tried to imagine who had painted
them, and under what circumstance. I imagined whoever created them never would have guessed that his
or her work would end up hidden between the studs
in a courthouse in a small Texas town. Life was full of
mysteries, I mused.

"Shame about Isabella," the mayor said out of the
blue. "Do you think she's the guilty party?"

"I don't know," I told her. "What do you know about
the Stones?"

"I know they've got bad luck as far as sons go," she
told me. "They'd better be good to Jenna; she's all
they've got left."

"Is there bad blood there?"

"Oh, everyone in town knows she was mad as a wet
hen when her brother came back into town to 'help
out' at the ranch."

"Did he have a good relationship with his parents?"

"I think on some level his daddy knew he was a bad egg," she said, "but his mother thought he walked on water. She's taken it real hard. Never wanted him to marry Isabella in the first place."

"Why?"

The mayor rolled her eyes. "She was still upset that Rhonda and Randy never got back together. Rhonda was Homecoming Queen back in her day, and I figger she thought a beauty queen of sorts would be just the right kind of mother to her grandchildren."

"She is an attractive young woman," I said. "But isn't there more to being a parent than looking good?"

"She's a nice young woman," the mayor said, "but still kind of lost, if you ask me. I'm glad she went to cosmetology school a few years back, but things seem to be going south for her. Then again, she was always the type to cause trouble."

"What do you mean?"

"She liked to stir up the boys," the mayor said. "Never happier than when she had two suitors arguin' over who'd get to take her to the dance."

"She had two boys lined up just recently," I said. "Think it was an accident she left that phone out for her husband to see?"

"Maybe," she mused. "Or maybe not. He's got a bad temper, Keith does."

"How did they meet?"

"In high school," she said. "He was on the football team. Always had a crush on Rhonda. Looked like the cat that ate the canary the day he finally got her to walk down the aisle with him. It must have just about killed him when he found out she was still seein' Randy Stone on the side."

"Well, somebody killed Randy," I pointed out. "Think it could be Keith Gehring?"

"He did have a temper," she said. "And it sure did look like a crime of passion. I might mention that to the deputy next time I see her."

"Is she taking over the case?"

"Rooster's convinced the case is closed," the mayor said. "No surprise. He likes things nice and easy. But things haven't been so easy for him lately."

"I know," I said, thinking it kind of served him right.

"It's kind of ironic, to my mind. All these years he's been shootin' himself in the foot figuratively, and he finally goes off and does it. I wouldn't be shocked if he ended up in the ER next time for trying to shove his foot down his throat." She grimaced. "Problem is, he doesn't know he's puttin' his foot in his mouth every time he talks. I wish we had someone else in that office, to be frank, but you know how traditions are."

"There's always been a Kocurek in the sheriff's office, hasn't there?"

"There has," she said. "But how many times do you have to mess up before someone shows you the door?" She shook her head.

"Well, I'm glad you won the last election," I said.

"So am I. Not for me... for Buttercup's sake," she said. "Can you imagine a freeway smack-dab through the middle of town?"

I could, but I didn't want to.

"Anyhow," she said, "I just wanted to show these to you. I guess I'd better put 'em back up."

"Let me help you," I said, reaching for the closest one. As I lifted it, something fluttered to the floor. I set down the painting and picked it up.

"What's that?" the mayor asked.

"A ticket, I think," I said, examining the scrap of card stock in my hand.

"What kind of ticket?"

"A movie ticket," I said. "Look; there's a date," I said, showing it to her.

"That's the day before the paintings were stolen. Is there a name?"

"Unfortunately, no," I said. "But it might be a lead. I doubt they'll have records of who bought tickets all those years ago, but you never know."

"Let's make a couple of copies of it," the mayor said. I handed it to her; a few minutes later, she returned and handed me one of the copies. "I'll hold on to the original and give it to whoever's still investigating the theft—or maybe to Deputy Shames—but in the meantime..."

"I'll see what I can find out," I promised. "Why Deputy Shames?"

She gave me a look. "Somebody's got to find out who was buried under the courthouse. Somethin' tells me Rooster's not the person to talk to about that."

"You think they're related?" I asked.

"I have no idea," she said. "That's for the police to figure out. It might lead them to the thief, the killer, the dead body... but it's not my department," she said.

I did a quick survey of the paintings to see if there was anything else wedged into the frames or the backings, but found nothing. "At least there aren't bloodstains!" I said cheerily.

"Thank heavens for small mercies," she said.

❧

By the time I got home, it would have been time to

turn around and head over to Opal's for the Buttercup Knitting Brigade. Unfortunately, there was no time to go if I wanted to get ready for the Christmas Market. As I started gathering merchandise for the Market, I called Opal to let her know.

"No worries," she said. "I'll stop by your booth with some cookies tonight."

"Thank you so much," I told her. "I also need some ideas for Tobias. I don't think I'm going to get this scarf done in time."

"I'll think on it," she said, and then in a lower voice, "Lord almighty. Flora just walked in looking like Glinda the Good Witch."

"You'll be able to talk her down," I said, grinning.

"Hope Gus likes middle-aged princesses," she said.

"He seems to so far," I said. "Check in with her, will you? Make sure she's not in over her head?"

"I will," she said. "See you tonight, and I'll think on what you can get Tobias!"

Speaking of Tobias, I thought as I hung up the phone, I still hadn't seen him since I got my hair cut. My hand reached up to touch my new hair again, and I resisted the urge to go look at my cut in the mirror again. Would he like it?

I'd find out soon enough, I told myself, forcing myself to focus on what needed to be done... and trying to come up with an idea for Tobias's Christmas present.

Chapter 13

THE MARKET WAS IN FULL swing by the time I got there, with one of the local church choirs singing carols, the scent of spices from the mulled mead and cider, and a hint of woodsmoke in the air. Even though the Market wasn't officially open yet, a throng of laughing, happy shoppers were swirling through the Square, dressed in jackets and brightly colored scarves and hats and checking out the locals' wares. It was a good thing it was only a couple more days until Christmas, I thought as I laid out my merchandise; although I'd been preparing for at least a month, I was starting to run low on stock.

I had just finished setting out the soaps when Flora floated up to the booth, wearing an enormous pink skirt and a blouse that looked like it had had an angry run-in with a BeDazzler. She was wearing the pink lipstick Opal had given her the other day; I guess she'd decided she should match her lips.

"Hey there," I said. "You're all gussied up. Where are you headed tonight?"

"Gus's taking me dancing," she said, her eyes sparkling. "I don't know how to dance—Mama didn't ever let me—but he says he'll teach me!"

I thought of Gus's stolid, slow-moving form. I'd never pegged him for a dancer, but people surprise me all the time. "That sounds like fun," I told her.

"Opal sent these for you," Flora said, digging a small box out of her purse. I opened it; it was filled with powdered-sugar-coated cookies. I took one and popped it into my mouth, where it promptly melted. So of course I had to grab another.

"What does Tobias think of your hair?" she asked.

I finished swallowing my second cookie before answering. "He hasn't seen it yet," I told her. As I answered, Jenna and her husband drifted by. I brushed off my fingers and put away the box of cookies. "Hi!" I said, overbrightly. Jenna looked up at me, and her face turned wary. "We met at your ranch the other day. How's the cow doing?"

"Better, thanks," she said tightly.

"Are these beeswax candles?" Simon asked, seemingly oblivious to her discomfort.

"They are," I said. "We met the other day at the ranch. I'm Lucy Resnick."

"I remember! Simon Flagg," he said in response. The name tickled something in my brain, but I couldn't place it; his name had probably been in the news at some point while I was working at the *Houston Chronicle*. A smile crossed his face; he was a handsome man, and seemed to be easy-going relative to the uptight vibe I got from Jenna. Then again, if he was a successful developer, he could just be good with people. "Did you make these yourself?" he asked, sniffing a candle.

"I did," I confirmed.

"Wow. I'd love a couple of these," he said. "I like candles, but the fake scents make me sneeze."

"I'd be happy to wrap them up for you," I said, and turned to Jenna. "I'm sorry about your brother, by the way. That's got to be rough on the family."

Jenna said nothing, but nodded shortly.

"Randy wasn't the best guy in the world, but he didn't deserve that," Simon answered for her. "It's ironic; Jenna was trying to convince me to move to Buttercup because it was safer. I'll be glad to get back to Houston!"

"You're not staying?" I asked.

"We'll be here through the holidays," he said, "try to help Jenna's parents get through, but after that, we're headed back home."

"Is that where you're from originally?"

He nodded. "I'm a city boy. Jenna here just loves being out in the country, though."

"I can relate to that," I said. "I left Houston myself."

"What brought you here?"

"The paper downsized and my grandmother's farm came up for sale. It was like it was meant to be," I said.

He frowned almost imperceptibly. "You were with the Houston paper?"

"I was," I said. "I was an investigative reporter."

"We have to hurry," Jenna said, touching his sleeve. "I promised to meet mother and daddy."

"Right," Simon said. "Anyway, what do I owe you?"

I told him, and he quickly shelled out a twenty from the thick wad in his billfold. "Keep the change," he said, and as I handed him the wrapped candles, he nodded and put a protective arm around Jenna, steering her away.

"He's handsome," Flora said as the trim couple disappeared into the crowd.

"He is," I agreed, running his name through my memory. I knew I'd encountered it before. But where?

"Not as handsome as Gus, though," Flora said. "I like beefy men." I smiled. It was a good thing; Gus definitely was a meat-and-potatoes kind of guy. "I just can't figure out what I should get him for Christmas. I want it to be special, but not too special."

"That's a tough one," I agreed. "It's hard when you start dating someone just before Christmas, or Valentine's Day. Maybe you could make him some cookies, or fudge, or something."

"That's an idea," she said, but didn't sound convinced. "How's your gift for Tobias coming?"

I groaned. "There's no way I'm going to get that scarf finished. Any other ideas for Christmas?"

She thought about it for a moment, and then her eyes lit up. "Ooh, I know!"

"What?" I asked, resisting the urge to reach for the cookies again.

"I saw an antique veterinary kit at Fannie's Antiques the other day," she said. "I actually talked about it with Fannie. It would be perfect for Tobias!"

It would; I knew he collected vintage veterinary equipment. "How much?" I asked.

She grimaced. "It wasn't cheap," she said. "But maybe she'd barter with you, or work out a deal."

I glanced over at Fannie's store. "Think she's still got it?"

"Go look," Flora urged me. "I'll get the rest of the booth set up."

"Thanks," I said, grabbing my purse and slinging it over my shoulder. "I'll be right back!"

Fannie's Antiques was in one of the long buildings that lined the Square. Fannie had decorated the front with vintage Christmas ornaments, Spode platters and cups, and a lovely live garland decorated with twinkling lights. The Market had drawn lots of potential shoppers; the store was lively, and I felt a twinge of nervousness in my stomach. What if someone had already bought it?

Fannie was busy wrapping up a vintage tree skirt for the woman at the register, but she waved to me when she spotted me. I scanned the festive, somewhat cluttered shop as she completed the transaction, feeling mounting anxiety. I didn't see anything even vaguely medical; there were hutches and pitchers and furniture, but no antique vet kits. "Have a wonderful holiday!" Fannie told the woman as she slid the tree skirt into a bag and handed it to her, then turned to me. "I'm so glad you made it in... I got the most amazing thing the other day, and I think Tobias would love it!"

"Flora told me," I said. "Do you still have it?"

"I do," she said. "Follow me." She squeezed out from behind the counter and led me to the back of the shop. She was wearing one of her vintage dresses, and her hair was pulled up into a loose bun; for a moment, I felt I had stepped back in time.

The feeling increased when she pulled a well-used black case from the shelf and opened it. The case was filled with metal instruments, including an enormous syringe, some kind of pink tubing, and even a green instruction booklet labeled "Easy-to-Use Cattle Instruments." "What is this?" I asked, touching the tubing.

"I have no idea, but I'll bet Tobias would know," she said. "He collects this stuff. Normally, I'd call him first thing, but with Christmas coming, I thought you might want to have first dibs."

"Oh, thank you so much. He'd love it," I said. "How much?"

"It's in such good shape I could probably get a pretty penny for it, but I picked it up for only fifty dollars. I normally ask double, but since you're local, how about seventy-five?"

"How about sixty and a couple of beeswax candles?" I asked.

"It's a deal; that'll make a great gift for my sister," she said.

I smiled, relieved I could give up on the scarf. Maybe in another three Christmases it would be ready, but life was just too busy for extended knitting for now. "I don't have the cash with me, but could you put it aside for me?"

"How about I stop by the booth at the end of the Market, and we can settle up then?"

"Actually, I'm hoping Tobias will be there," I said. "Can you hold on to it for me? I'll come pick it up tomorrow."

"My pleasure," she said. "I'm glad it's going to such a good home."

I stepped out of the shop feeling much lighter. I hadn't realized how worried I'd been about finishing Tobias's scarf. I loved giving handmade things, but I had a feeling that with the amount of cold weather we got in Texas, there wouldn't be too many opportunities for it to be worn. Besides, I had a feeling the antique veterinary kit would be a more special gift.

I was still in good spirits as I wove through the Christmas Market. I was considering splurging on a cone of candied almonds when raised voices caught my attention.

"Your daughter killed my son!" It was a woman's voice, filled with rage and loss. I hurried over to where a crowd of onlookers had gathered. Linda Stone stood, face almost purple, pointing a finger at an equally stricken looking woman I recognized as Mandy's mother, Valeria Vargas.

"Your son didn't deserve my daughter. But she did not lay a finger on him. Maybe it was one of his hussies... or one of their husbands who did it!" Valeria yelled back. "My daughter is innocent." Mandy stood next to her, looking fretful, and was talking into her ear, though she wasn't listening.

"Then what is she doing sitting in jail?" Linda shot back. "I knew he should have married Rhonda. Knew it. But once your girl got her claws into him, everything went downhill. His life was never the same after that."

"Oh, please. If it weren't for Isabella, they would have lost the house six months ago. I don't like to speak ill of the dead, but your son was a worthless, cheating layabout. I wish my daughter had never laid eyes on him."

Before Randy's mother could respond, Mayor Niederberger stepped in. "Now, now. I know things are hot right now, and there's been a lot of tragedy, but let's not talk about it here, okay?"

"But..."

"I know, Linda. It's been a terrible time for you. But this isn't going to help anything." She looked over at William Stone, who was standing there with a stricken look on his broad face. "Billy, why don't you take her over to that bench on the green to cool down?" Without waiting for him to act, she turned to Valeria. "I know it's been a horrible shock this week. The police are still working on the case... and so's Lucy here," she added, throwing me under the bus.

Valeria's eyes lit up. "Lucy? You don't believe it either?"

"I'm helping Mandy try to figure out what happened," I said in a low voice, aware of about fifty pairs of listening ears. I walked over and took Valeria gently by the elbow. "I'd love to talk with you, though. Why don't you and Mandy come with me?"

She acquiesced, and walked with me, still sobbing, toward my booth. Mandy walked with me for a little bit, then excused herself. "I've got a few more things to take care of for the paper," she told me. "I'll come find you at the booth."

"I've got her," I promised. "I'll keep her at the booth."

"Thanks," Mandy said, and hurried away.

"I just can't believe my baby's in jail," Valeria wailed as I tried to shield her from onlookers; she seemed unaware that Mandy had left. "She was the sweetest girl; she would never do something as brutal as that."

I guided her to my booth, then sat her down on one of the folding chairs I'd brought with me, back and away from the main booth. Flora nodded and continued to woman the booth while I took care of Valeria, pulling up a chair next to her and rubbing her back while she sobbed. "What was going on between them recently?" I asked gently.

"Oh, same as always. He couldn't keep a job. Drank all their money away. I think he was counting on that inheritance, and just biding his time until the money came through."

"Was the ranch coming to him?"

She nodded. "It was supposed to, eventually. I know his sister was hoping for it, but he always talked about what he'd do when the ranch was his." She rolled her eyes. "Run it into the ground, most likely."

"He wasn't the best businessman in the world, I gather."

"If it weren't for Isabella's job, they'd be out on the street. As it was, we helped them a few times. Last time, though, Isabella told him to ask his parents instead."

"And they gave him a job back at the ranch?"

"Well, that's what Randy said, but you couldn't believe anything from his mouth. When Isabella suspected he was still sweet on Rhonda, he told her she was crazy, that there was nothing between Rhonda and him." She wiped her eyes. "And it turns out he was back here romancing her the whole time."

"When did she find out?"

"Rhonda's husband Keith called and told her. And then she looked on his computer, and found they'd been talking for months. And there were pictures, too." She buried her head in her arms, and I made soothing noises until she got herself back together.

"That sounds horrible," I said. "He wasn't a very nice man, was he?"

"Not at all," she said, weeping. "He made enemies everywhere he went. He got fired a few weeks ago."

Before I could say anything else, Tobias appeared.

"Hey," I said, smiling at him.

"Your hair looks terrific," he said right away. I raised my hand to my hair; I'd almost forgotten about it.

"Thanks," I told him. "This is Mandy and Isabella's mother, Valeria. Valeria, this is Tobias."

"I've seen you at Rosita's," he said. "I'm sorry about all the family trouble."

"Me too," she said in a voice so full of loss it hurt my heart. As I reached out to squeeze her shoulder, a scream sounded from the other end of the Market.

"Stay here," I told her, and ran over toward the source of the scream, with Tobias at my side.

Chapter 14

IT CAME FROM THE RESTROOMS near the court-house. Three people were standing near the small building, their hands to their mouths.

"What is it?" Tobias asked.

"It's... I went in to use the bathroom," the girl closest to the door said, "and she was in there, on the floor!"

"I'll go look," I told Tobias. After all, it was the ladies' room.

I pulled open the door and stepped inside. Lying on the floor next to one of the stalls was Julie, the young waitress I'd talked with at Rosita's. I hurried over and checked her pulse; there was nothing, and her chest was motionless.

"Tobias," I called. "I need you."

The door burst open, and he came through. "No pulse," I told him. "And I don't think she's breathing."

"No," he said. "She's not. Call 911," he said as he did a thorough inspection of the young woman and rolled her over. I pulled my phone out of my pocket and called, but I somehow knew it would be too late; and as soon as I saw the other side of Julie, I realized I was right.

We now had two murders in Buttercup the week before Christmas.

"I feel terrible," I said as we waited outside the bathrooms for the paramedics to do their job. "She was going to tell me something about Randy the other day, but she didn't get a chance. If I'd gone back and asked, maybe this wouldn't have happened."

"When did that happen?"

"When I was making tamales at Rosita's," I said. "She saw him come back to the restaurant that night and argue with Isabella."

"What else did she see?"

"She told me she saw Isabella leave, but she was angry."

"This was in the middle of the night, right? What was she doing there?"

The thought had crossed my mind, too. "Do you think she was meeting Randy for a tryst? That would point to jealousy as the motive for murder."

"Only Isabella's in jail."

"Well, that's one saving grace, at least. She won't be charged with two murders."

Tobias grimaced. "Wasn't that her mom you were just talking to?"

I hadn't made that connection yet. "You don't think she killed her?"

"She knew her," Tobias pointed out. "They both worked at the restaurant; Valeria was her boss, really."

"But to stab her with a knife at the Christmas Market... I just can't see her doing that."

"Maybe not," he said. "But I don't want you alone with her. In fact, until we figure this out, I don't want you alone with anyone."

We stood in silence for a moment, and he put an arm

around me. "She was just about to tell me something about Randy—Mr. Stone, she called him—when Mandy showed up, so she stopped talking."

"Any idea what it might have been about?"

I shook my head. "I can't even remember what we'd been talking about, to be honest. It's been a whirlwind of a week."

"Still no sign of Rhonda?"

"No," I said. "But I really do think she was the person I saw at the guest house. I went to the salon she works at today, and she talked with one of the other stylists. Said she was going to be out of town for a while, had somewhere to stay. The stylist said it sounded fishy, but she didn't know what Rhonda was doing."

"What would she be doing at the Stones' house, though? I mean, if Randy was still alive, I could see it, but why would anyone else want her there?"

"I don't know," I said. "I don't even know for sure that she's there. I wish there were some way to find out."

"I have to go back to check on that cow tomorrow," he said. "Why don't you come with me?"

"Wouldn't that seem too weird?"

"I don't really care," he said, pulling me in to him. "You're my girlfriend. It's the holiday season. We like to hang out together."

"Thanks," I said, feeling warm all over. "I needed to hear that."

"I know it's not a good time," he said. "But we should probably talk about Christmas sometime soon."

"Probably," I said, feeling apprehensive again. "Do you have plans?"

Before he could answer, Deputy Shames called to us. "You're the ones who found her?"

"Actually, it was this young woman here," I said, indicating the huddle of teenagers not far from the bathroom door. "We went in to see if there was anything we could do."

"What time was that?"

"About thirty minutes ago, I'd say." I glanced at my watch and realized I'd left Flora alone the whole night, and that as far as I knew, Valeria was still sitting on a chair in the back of the booth. I knew Flora was supposed to have a date with Gus; I needed to get back to spell her. "Do you mind if I head back to my booth? I've got a helper there, but I think she's got somewhere to go."

"That's fine," she said, "but please stick around until I've had a chance to talk to you. Dr. Brandt, can I ask you a few questions in the meantime?"

"Of course," he said, giving me a peck on the cheek and squeezing my hand. "I'll be over in a few," he promised, and I hurried back to the booth.

Flora seemed to be doing just fine without me, although she was full of questions. Mandy's mother, I noticed, was no longer at the booth. "Where did Valeria go?" I asked.

"She went to get some nuts after you left," Flora told me. "Mandy came looking for her, too. What happened?"

"There was another murder," I told her. I realized I hadn't seen Mandy; that was a bit surprising, because she was the editor of the *Buttercup Zephyr*. "A young woman. She worked as a waitress at Rosita's."

Flora's eyes widened. "But Isabella's in jail! She couldn't have done it!"

"No," I said. "She couldn't have." But Mandy could. Had my friend killed Randy to protect her sister... and then done in Julie to cover her tracks? I didn't like thinking about it, but I had to consider it.

Although carols still played and shoppers drifted by, the holiday feel had gone from the evening for me. Not so much for Flora, though, who was in the throes of early love.

"He wants to spend Christmas with me," she said. "Can you believe it? We've only been dating a few days, and he's going to have me over for a full Christmas dinner!"

"That's great," I said, trying to muster enthusiasm. I was happy for her, but I had other things on my mind. "Where does he live, anyway?"

"Out off of 71, on the way to La Grange."

"Take your time," I said.

"I'll try," she said. "But sometimes things are just meant to be, you know?"

I hoped she was right.

Tobias and I had parted ways after the Market, the topic of Christmas no longer on either of our minds. I went home and did my chores, then slept fitfully, the scene at Rosita's replaying in my dreams. Why hadn't I gone to talk to Julie earlier?

And was it really possible my friend was a killer?

That was the thought that kept sneaking into my mind as I took care of all the animals and checked the rows of baby lettuces and broccoli the next morning. It was cold and clear, and the sky was a deep, pristine blue above the bleached gold of the fields. There had been a frost the night before, and the grass crackled as I walked on it. I took a deep breath of the frosty air, which was laced with a touch of woodsmoke. It brought back wonderful memories of Christmas on the farm as a girl. Serafine had told me that my grandmother was still here, looking after me. I hadn't felt her presence in a while, but now, for just a moment, I thought I detected a touch of her rose scent on a stray breeze. "I miss you, Grandma," I said, hoping she could somehow hear me.

There was no answer, of course, but I felt better for saying it, and turned to check on the goats and cows, who all looked very anxious to see me. I fed everyone carrots and praised them for not heading down to the Christmas Market to eat candied almonds again this year, then fed and watered my small flock of chickens, who weren't looking very happy about the cold weather. As I finished gathering eggs—only two this morning—I paused, looking down at the little house on the knoll. It looked picture-perfect from where I stood; for a moment, I could see what it would look like when the renovations were done.

If they were done.

Again, that scent of rose on the breeze. I smiled, feeling my grandmother's encouragement. "Thank you," I told her, and headed into the house. If only I could ask her who the murderer was, I thought. Although I wasn't sure I'd like the answer.

I was still thinking about the unsolved murders when I finished cleaning up my breakfast dishes. The first death had taken place at Rosita's, and both murders had Rosita's in common. Something told me Rosita's—or somebody at Rosita's—was likely at the center of them.

I'd been planning on making a batch of candy cane fudge but decided I'd come back and do that later in the day; right now, I thought a breakfast taco would be just the thing.

Even if I'd just finished breakfast.

It was a pleasant drive to Rosita's; the sky was still that deep, cerulean blue, and the houses, with their wreaths on the doors and garlands and ribbons festooning their front porches, were a lovely reminder of the season. We might not have much snow in Texas, but Texans certainly enjoyed decorating for the holiday. The mistletoe had sold out again last night. Which made me think of the mistletoe in Randy's hair. Where had it come from? Had someone put it there as a decoy, or had he been somewhere else right before he got to Rosita's? Maybe with someone else?

I wasn't sure how I was going to find out any answers, but I'd do my best . And if nothing else, I decided, at least I'd pick up a tub of salsa.

Rosita's was crowded as usual when I pulled into the parking lot. I recognized the town librarian heading out to her truck with a big bag of either tamales or breakfast tacos, and I could hear the bustle even before I got to the door.

A young woman I didn't recognize was at the counter. "Can I help you?" she asked.

I surveyed the busy restaurant, which was filled with gossip. It seemed the recent goings-on involving Rosita's had been excellent for business.

"Table for one, please," I said.

"It'll be about five minutes," she told me. "We're

busy this morning."

"I can see," I told her, glancing down at the plastic name tag pinned to her shirt. "Camille, right? I'm Lucy Resnick. I'm sorry about the loss of one of your coworkers."

Her mouth drooped. "Yeah. It's creepy. We were friends."

"Were you?" I asked. "Do you have any idea what happened?"

She shook her head. "I was supposed to meet her at the Market; we were going to go shopping for our families. But by the time I got there, she was gone." Her eyes grew shiny with tears.

"That's awful," I said. "It's hard to believe anyone would do something like that."

"I know," she said, swiping at her eyes. "I mean, what did anyone have to gain? She was a waitress; she didn't have tons of money. She was going to go to school for accounting in the spring. And now..." She took a deep breath. "I'm sorry."

"There's no need to be sorry," I said. "It's a loss. Did Julie have family, a boyfriend..."

"She has... had a boyfriend. I don't think they were that serious, though. I think she was seeing someone else, too."

"A few days ago, when I was here helping make tamales, she was going to tell me something about Randy Stone, but someone interrupted us. She didn't happen to mention anything to you, did she?"

She hesitated for a moment before shaking her head. "No," she said, but her face looked more guarded.

"Look," I said quietly, leaning over the counter. "If you know something about Randy, you should tell me. I'm not sure why someone killed Julie, but it might have something to do with what she was going to tell me but didn't. Please...just tell me."

She took a deep breath and seemed to be debating what to do. Then, after a moment, she let out a long breath. "She was seeing him. Mr. Stone."

I blinked. "What?"

"They were seeing each other," she said.

"Oh, man. That explains it."

"What?"

"She said she was in the parking lot the night Randy died," I said in a low voice. "I wondered why she'd be here; now it makes sense. She told me she was calling her sister."

The young woman rolled her eyes. "She was here to meet him, I'll bet. They used to make out in his truck, she told me. Sometimes in the restaurant, too." She made a face. "It's kind of gross, really. She had a nice boyfriend, but she really had the hots for Randy." She teared up again. "I always thought he was a jerk, but she just didn't see it. Do you think that's why she died? Because she got involved with him?"

"I don't know," I answered, but I thought the odds were pretty good. "Did she ever say anything about him?"

She bit her lip. "Only that he drank a lot," she said. "And that he was a good kisser."

"Anything else?"

"He talked a lot about how he was going to run the ranch," she said. "How it was all going to be his one day. His sister was trying to drive him out of the business, but he needed it more than she did. That he *deserved* it."

"I heard she has an MBA."

"I heard that, too."

"What about Randy?"

She shook her head. "Not that I know of." As she spoke, a crowd of people came through the door behind me. Camille gave me a faint smile. "I'll let you know when your table's ready," she said, and turned to help the next people in line.

I retreated to a seat close to the door and waited, thinking about what she had just told me. Who wasn't Randy Stone seeing? I wondered. I only knew about the women in Buttercup. Were there more in Katy, where he and Isabella had a house?

I knew one thing for sure: The more I found out about Randy Stone, the less I liked him.

My waitress was nice, but not particularly forthcoming with juicy details. When I got my table, I ordered a *papas*, egg, and cheese taco, and ate it with some of the restaurant's famed Salsa Doña, then excused myself to visit the ladies' room, which was next to the kitchen.

I was about to go in when the door to the kitchen opened. I glanced inside and spotted something I hadn't seen before; hanging over the tortilla maker was a sprig of mistletoe. And it looked as if a piece of it had been torn off.

The door closed again, leaving me wondering.

Had Randy and Julie had an assignation here before he died?

And had Julie died because she'd seen Randy's murder?

Chapter 15

I WAS STILL UNSETTLED WHEN I swung by the Honeyed Moon Mead Winery a half hour later; I needed to pick up some more beeswax for candles.

Serafine was busy wrapping gifts when I arrived, listening to jazzy Christmas carols as she worked.

"Come in, come in!" she invited me. "I was just wrapping up a couple of things for Aimee.... She went out for a few hours, so I grabbed the opportunity." I stepped into her home, which was filled with memorabilia from her native New Orleans, along with a variety of unusual handmade things that looked distinctly magical. She was, in fact, a practicing witch, so they probably were.

"What did you end up getting her?"

"Some handmade earrings I found at the Market last night," she said, "and a beautiful hand-painted silk scarf. I wrapped the scarf, but these are the earrings. You think she'll like them?"

"They're gorgeous," I said as she lifted two chandelier earrings. They were silver filigree with ruby-red crystals that glowed and sparkled in the light.

"You think? I hope so."

"I'm sure she will," I said. "What are you two doing for Christmas?"

"We're heading home to visit family," she said. "We're

leaving tomorrow."

"I guess you don't have livestock to take care of."

She grinned. "Nope. The bees kinda take care of themselves, thank goodness. Speaking of bees, the beeswax candles are really selling fast, eh?" she asked. Her hair was done up in a gorgeous blue and green scarf, and with the crystals sparkling at her throat, she looked like an enchantress of sorts.

"They are," I said. "I won't have time to cure the new ones completely, but I can tell folks how to care for them. I'm just about out of stock."

"Maybe you'll need more than one hive, then," she suggested.

"I'm going to start small," I told her. "I don't want to get in over my head. Or more over my head."

She laughed. "We're all in over our heads. Sometimes I think I'm crazy for moving to Buttercup. Other times, I wonder what took me so long."

"I totally get that," I replied, smiling.

"Come with me," she said, slipping on a pair of rubber boots that looked out of keeping with her skinny jeans and loose, sparkly top. Together, we left the house and headed for the barn where she kept her beeswax and made mead. "I've got several blocks left; someone got in touch online and asked if she could buy a huge bulk order the other day, but I knew you'd need more, so I saved some back."

"Thank you," I said. "Before I leave, remind me; I brought you a bit of fresh arugula and some radishes; I'll have another batch of lettuce ready next week." I'd harvested some and put it in a bag in the truck before heading to Rosita's.

"Oh, that sounds divine. I love winter arugula; it's got a bit of a bite, but nothing like hot-weather greens." As we walked to the barn, she gave me a sidelong look. "You're upset about something."

"Is it that obvious?"

She nodded. "Completely. It's about those deaths, isn't it?"

"It is," I said. "Randy Stone just seems like a horrible guy; he was entangled with women left and right," I said. "And now Julie, too. I found out she was seeing him on the side; they met at Rosita's the night he died."

"No wonder he had mistletoe in his hair," Serafine said.

"Is that bit of info out and about?"

"It's Buttercup, buttercup. Not a lot of secrets. Although Randy Stone did a good job of it. And boy, did his momma and daddy name him right." She grinned as she unlocked the barn. Most folks didn't lock their barns, but with teenagers in town and cases of mead inside, Serafine was cautious.

I laughed despite myself as she opened the door, letting out a waft of honey-sweet, warm air. "I just wish I could figure out what this was about."

Serafine got a misty look and froze, her hand still on the barn door. "It's not about love," she said suddenly.

A chill rose up my spine that had nothing to do with the temperature. "What is it, then?" I asked.

"It's... it's dark. And angry."

"Couldn't that be a jilted lover?"

"I do have the feeling of betrayal," she said. "But it doesn't feel like a crime of passion. Not that kind of passion, anyway." She was quiet for another moment. "There's something old in there, too. Something unresolved, from years and years ago."

I thought of Randy's disappearing brother. "Does it have something to do with Randy's missing older brother?" I asked.

She narrowed her eyes. "Yes. And no." She stood motionless for another moment, then shook herself. "It's gone," she said, and her whole manner changed.

"You can't call whatever it is back?"

"That's not how it works, unfortunately," she said, opening the barn door the rest of the way. Together, we stepped inside, and she flipped on the light. The room was filled with brewing equipment, glass containers of honey-colored liquid, and hundreds of bottles.

"I've got to tell you, the spirit world could stand to be a little clearer."

"Tell me about it," she said.

"So, it's not a jilted lover," I said. "Which rules out Rhonda's husband, assuming we can count on the spirit world, that is. But it is about betrayal... and something to do with his missing brother."

"He disappeared a long time ago, didn't he?" she asked. "I got a feeling of tragedy. I don't think he's alive anymore."

"I don't know if that would be good news or bad news for his parents," I said. "It's got to be awful living without closure for all those years."

"Yes," she said. "I feel like his mother in particular has suffered a lot. So sad," she said with a sigh. "And now two more deaths."

"Any word from the other side on Rhonda Gehring?" I asked. After all, why not?

"No," she said, shaking her head. "Only that I don't think she's passed."

"Good," I said. I didn't share that I had a feeling I knew where she was.

"There's something else about her, though... I can't put a finger on it," she said a moment later.

"Well, she did just lose her lover and is probably about to get divorced."

"That, too, but I'm getting something different. Something's starting for her. Something she's not sure about." I thought about the venture Sadie had thought sounded "fishy," and wondered if that was what Serafine was referring to. I waited, hoping for more, but my friend's shoulders drooped and she shook her head. "It's gone again, I'm afraid. But it's a big ol' mess. And there may be more death waiting."

"More? We've already had two deaths and one missing person. How much more can there be?"

"You'll just have to solve it, then," she said, giving me a smile. "I think that's why the spirits spoke up. They're counting on you."

Terrific. Not only was Mandy counting on me, but now everyone on the other side was, too. "I moved to Buttercup to get away from investigative reporting," I complained.

"Unfortunately, it followed you, it seems," Serafine said. She waited a moment, head cocked, looking as if she was listening, then shrugged. "Nothing else, at least not today."

"You'll call me if you get anything?" I asked. I might be an investigative reporter, but I wouldn't say no to a bit of guidance, whether it came from this world or the next.

"I will," she said, "but I get the feeling they're done for the day. Anyway, let's get you that beeswax," she said, suddenly all business again.

"Thanks," I said, but my thoughts were still with that weird interlude. Betrayal, but not in the context of a love affair. And something to do with an old tragedy.

This case was getting stranger and more convoluted

by the minute.

❧

It was almost noon by the time I pulled into the driveway to Dewberry Farm, a box of beeswax on the seat next to me and a few bags of groceries I'd picked up at the Red and White Grocery. I'd remembered to give the veggies to Serafine, who planned to take them home to New Orleans with her, and had decided that I needed to get going and make some fudge for my many friends in Buttercup. I still wanted to try the recipe Tracy had given me for candy cane fudge, so I decided to stop at the store to pick up the ingredients and spend the afternoon making a massive batch. My friends and I usually exchanged food gifts or home-made items rather than store-bought stuff, but I was a bit behind this year and needed to get on the stick.

I put the box of beeswax on the counter and said hello to Chuck, who was wagging so hard his whole body was rocking from side to side, and then headed back out to get the groceries. As I unloaded the bags from the truck and then pulled a big pot out of the cabinet, I reflected on everything I now knew about Randy's murder.

The mistletoe in his hair had probably come from Rosita's, I now knew, and he more than likely had had an assignation with Julie that night. Had Isabella come and interrupted them? Was that why she was so loath to say where she'd been? Had she, in fact, killed Randy out of anger and jealousy?

But if so, why hadn't Julie said anything about it to the police? She had a boyfriend, but she wasn't married, so she didn't have that much to lose. Still, if Isabella had walked in on them, it certainly gave her a motive to murder both Randy and Julie.

But Isabella was in jail when Julie was murdered.

Was it Mandy who'd done it?

As I put the white chocolate chips and the sweetened condensed milk into the pot on the stove, I reflected once again on what Serafine had told me. The deaths had been about betrayal, not passionate love. Was it possible Isabella had killed Randy out of anger, and Julie was murdered by Mandy to protect her sister? Mandy hadn't been around when the body was found, which was weird for the editor of a paper. Was that because she was responsible?

I didn't like anything about this case, I decided as I lined two pans with foil and sprayed them with cooking spray. And Randy cheating on his wife had absolutely nothing to do with his missing brother, which Serafine had intimated had something to do with the present-day murder. I gave the pot a stir, then unwrapped some candy canes and put them into a Ziploc bag before gently tapping them with a mallet.

I crushed candy canes and stirred the pot until the contents had melted into a sweet, white liquid, then checked the recipe card. I took it off the heat and added the peppermint extract, some of the crushed candy canes, and a dash of red food coloring. , I poured it into the pans, trying to make it even, and then sprinkled crushed candy canes on top.

The fudge looked beautiful and smelled enticing; I couldn't wait to try it. I took a little sample from the side of the pot, hoping it wouldn't be grainy; to my relief, it was smooth and minty and delicious. I cleaned out the rest of the pot with a spatula, nibbling on bits of half-cured fudge as I cleaned, and then started the process over, only with the semisweet chocolate.

Twenty minutes later, I had four pans of beautiful fudge, two white chocolate mint and two milk chocolate mint, and had snacked my way to being almost full. It was an amazing recipe, creamy and minty, with a nice crunch from the candy canes. I'd have to thank Tracy when I saw her.

As I dried the pot and put it up in the cabinet, I spotted the copy of the ticket; I'd stuck it to the fridge with a magnet. I took it down and examined it. It was a movie theater ticket from Houston... which was where the paintings had been stolen from.

I looked at the date, and an idea popped into my head. I opened my laptop, pulled up the museum's name, and typed in "Art Theft." Sure enough, three articles on the missing paintings turned up; they'd disappeared the day after the date on the move ticket. Then I pulled up the *Buttercup Zephyr* website. Mandy had been having back issues scanned to cut down on storage, which made things convenient for me; right now, I wasn't sure I wanted to go ask her for anything.

I input the date on the ticket. There was nothing that day. An update on the courthouse renovations, which I hadn't realized had been going on for coming up on two decades, a small article about a herd of escaped cows mowing down the flowers in front of the Red and White Grocery, which made me feel much better about my own occasional wayward livestock—and an article predicting a droughty summer. Some things never change, I thought, and flipped on the previous week's edition.

And that's when things got interesting.

Five days before the date on the ticket we'd found in the back of the painting, Chad Stone disappeared.

Which gave me a very bad feeling about the bones beneath the courthouse.

Chapter 16

I READ THE ARTICLE TWICE. THERE was a photo of Chad, who resembled his brother but with longer hair, that looked like it had come from a high-school yearbook. Chad Stone had been a member of 4-H and a bit of a track star in Buttercup, specializing in hurdles; it read more like an obituary, in some ways, than a missing persons article. Apparently, he'd started school at the University of Houston, studying management, but I got the feeling he hadn't completed his studies.

There was a picture of Linda and William Stone on an inside page. Linda Stone had aged tremendously in the past fifteen years... probably the toll of grief. William looked much the same, stoic and solid, his mouth a grim line. "I just want my boy back," he was quoted as saying. "I haven't slept in days. He was going to Houston for a job, and then... he just never called." According to the article, Chad had checked out of the hotel he was staying in and just disappeared. No phone calls, no nothing.

"We're offering a reward," William Stone said. "Anyone who knows anything about what might have happened to our son, please let us know."

I took one last look at the photo of Linda and William, standing in front of their house, looking bereft, and my heart ached for them. They'd lost both their sons. That wasn't how things were supposed to happen.

I scrolled through the next few weeks of the paper, looking for more information. There were a few update articles, but no new information on Chad, and despite the generous reward information—they were offering $50,000 to anyone who could find their missing boy—the story just kind of faded out as time went on. At least in the paper. I was sure it was just as current for the Stones as it was when their son had first disappeared.

I leaned back, staring at the computer. If I was right about what had happened, how had Chad Stone gotten involved in an art theft? And if he had, were those his bones that had been found in the courthouse? I flipped back to the article on the renovation. They'd ripped up part of the floor because of a water leak, apparently, and taken out some rotten drywall. What had made Chad decide to come back to Buttercup to stash the paintings? And who had done it with him?

And then, I thought to myself, probably done him in?

I picked up the phone to call Tobias. He answered on the second ring. "Hey, Lucy. What's up?"

"I was wondering if you'd been out to check on the Stones' cow yet," I said.

"I scheduled the recheck for this afternoon. I take it you'd like to come with me?"

"I would," I said.

"I'll pick you up at noon, then," he told me.

"Looking forward to it."

❧

Tobias showed up just before twelve. I'd finished

packing up the fudge and watered all the greens, which were thriving in the cooler weather. Texas had two growing seasons: the hot season, which involved cucumbers, tomatoes, eggplants, and peppers, and the cool one, which was when leafy greens, beets, radishes, and cruciferous vegetables flourished. I'd planted onions and potatoes this year, too, and was looking forward to freshly dug new potatoes with homemade butter.

"Wow," he said when he saw me. "I keep forgetting about your haircut; it really does look great on you!"

"Thanks," I said, blushing. "I'm still getting used to it."

"You know I think you're gorgeous no matter what your hair looks like, don't you?"

My heart just about melted in my chest as he gave me a kiss and ran a hand through my hair. "Feels silky, too."

"Sadie talked me into buying some new shampoo," I said. "We'll see what it looks like after I'm done with it."

"Like I said, Lucy: gorgeous." He gave me another quick kiss before squatting down to pet Chuck. As he distributed belly rubs, I grabbed a box of fudge and reached for my boots. "That fudge looks good," he said, looking up at the clear container in my hand. "Is it for me?"

"No," I said. "Not this box, anyway; I'm taking it to the Stones."

"Any news on what happened to Randy?" he asked.

"Not yet, but I think I know what happened to their missing son," I told him.

He blinked. "What?"

As we walked out of the farmhouse toward his truck,

I told him about the ticket I'd found tucked into the back of the painting, the date of the theft, and the timing of Chad Stone's disappearance.

"So it looks like he left town to commit art theft," Tobias said. "Who did he do it with?"

"That's the question, isn't it?" I mused as Tobias opened the truck door for me. I thanked him and clambered up into the cab, then put the fudge on my lap. "I'm guessing whoever it was probably committed the murder."

He closed the door and rounded the truck. As he climbed in next to me, he asked, "But why didn't they come back for the paintings?"

"Something must have happened to him," I speculated. "Or her."

"How does all of this relate to what happened to Randy Stone, do you think? Or Julie?"

"I don't know," I said. "I was hoping we could talk to his parents to find out who he was in contact with before he left... or what he told them, if anything."

"It was a long time ago. Do you think they'll remember?"

"I'm sure of it," I said. "I'll bet they remember every detail associated with his disappearance."

"Are you going to tell them your theory?"

"I don't know if I should," I said.

"They could do DNA testing."

"That's true," I said. "I hate to dredge it up right now... they just lost their other son." I bit my lip as we bumped down the driveway to the road. "I wish I knew if it really was Rhonda I saw there the other day. I'm almost sure it was; I just can't figure out what she's doing there."

"It's all a tangled mess, it seems. I still can't think why

anyone would have wanted to kill that poor young woman."

"I have an idea, but it's not one I like."

Tobias glanced over at me. "What are you thinking?"

"I'm thinking Isabella may have killed Randy when she caught him cheating, unfortunately. I know she was there. Julie saw her there. Remember? She was going to tell me something at Rosita's, but before I could find out what it was, someone killed her."

"How was she involved?"

"She was seeing Randy Stone secretly," I told him.

"That guy got around!" he said. "But if Isabella was in jail last night, who killed Julie?"

"I'm afraid it might have been Mandy," I said, with a sinking feeling in my stomach.

"I don't like it, but it makes sense," he said.

"She disappeared before we found Julie," I told him. "And she wasn't around at the scene of the crime."

"Maybe there's an innocent explanation," Tobias countered.

"Maybe," I said. "And none of this explains where Rhonda went. Or, if she's at the Stones' ranch, why she's there."

"What are you planning to do when we get there?" Tobias asked.

"Give them fudge. And wing it."

"I like your plan," he said, laughing, and reached over to squeeze my hand.

"Let's hope it works," I replied.

William Stone was waiting by the barn for us when we arrived, looking even grimmer than ever. When we got out of the truck, he flicked a brief glance in my direction before focusing on Tobias. "She's in here," he said, turning without more of a greeting and leading the way to the barn.

"I'll be right in," Tobias said. "Lucy brought you some fudge; is Mrs. Stone at home?"

"She is," he said curtly. "You can go knock on the door."

"Thanks," I said, trying not to feel offended—grief did funny things to people—and headed toward the main house, passing once again the Christmas decoration with Santa's list on it. Poor William and Linda Stone. Only one of those three children remained.

The heavy wood door was decorated with a big Christmas wreath covered in silver-gold ribbon and a few gold angels. I rang the doorbell, feeling trepidation; a moment later, Linda answered, her eyes red from crying.

"Hi," I said. "I'm sorry to intrude, but Dr. Brandt is here checking on one of the cows, and I came along for the ride."

"How nice," she said, putting on a brittle smile. "Can I get you a cup of coffee or a glass of tea?" she asked, Southern hospitality a reflex response.

"I'd love a cup of coffee," I said, and she invited me into the house. "I brought this for you," I told her, proffering the fudge. "I never got a chance to tell you how sorry I am for your loss."

She stifled a sob and took a deep breath, then took the box without looking at it. "That's two boys I've lost now," she said. "All I have left is Jenna."

"I'm so sorry," I said as she offered me a seat at her big oak kitchen table and retrieved a mug from one of the white-painted cabinets.

"I just kind of wonder what the point is these days," she said, her eyes straying to a picture of two boys and a girl, all smiling and full of life. "We're supposed to go first, not the other way around."

"I know," I said softly. I looked around the kitchen; it was filled with decorations that clearly had had meaning for the family. An old homemade felt Advent calendar hung on the wall next to the door, but only a few of the pins had been attached to the tree. A tree stood in the corner of the living room, with a hand-embroidered tree skirt around the base. It was decorated with ornaments that had clearly been hand-made by her children, and pictures of all three of her kids lined the walls. Although the decor was festive, the house was steeped in sadness and loss. The air felt so heavy it was almost hard to breathe.

"Thank you," I said as she handed me a cup of coffee. She didn't ask if I wanted cream or sugar, but frankly, I didn't care. I took a sip; it was dark and a few hours old, but that was fine. I wasn't here for coffee.

"You were with that hussy's mother last night," Linda said as she sat down, the polite, controlled veneer cracking a bit. "Are you on their side?"

"I'm not on anyone's side," I said. "Just the side of the truth."

She looked at me for a moment, then nodded and took a sip of her own murky coffee. I took that as permission to continue with caution. "I know this is a delicate subject right now," I said, "but have you heard about the paintings that were found in the court-house?"

She nodded, looking down at her hands, which were wrapped around her mug. "I have."

"I found a movie ticket in the back of one of them,"

I said. "I hate to bring this up, but it's from a few days after your first son disappeared."

She looked up, and the color leached from her face. "What?"

Chapter 17

"I THINK YOUR SON MAY HAVE been connected with those paintings," I told her. "I want to know if you remember anything about who he went with or where he was planning to go when he went to Houston."

"You think... you think he was an art thief?"

"I don't know," I said. "I'm just trying to put the pieces together."

"He was going to Houston for a job," she said, her eyes unfocused, as if she were in another time and place. "Said he was going to meet up with some guy who had a job for him. He went to school for management, but the university wasn't the right place for him. He was miserable."

"Was he moving to Houston, or did he say he'd be back?"

"He didn't know. He hoped he'd be staying. The man he was working with was called Sparky."

"Sparky?"

She nodded. "I know; it was a weird name. I wasn't very comfortable with it, but I talked it over with Bill, and what could we do?"

"How did he meet this guy?"

"When he was at school in Houston. He never told me how; I got the impression it was another student, but he didn't say much. And then it was too late..." She trailed off, and then a look of horror crossed her face. "There were bones in the courthouse," she said. "Oh, no... please, no..."

"We don't know anything about those yet," I said, reaching out and putting a hand on her arm.

"But... why would he come back to Buttercup? It doesn't make sense."

"I don't know that either," I said. "And it's just a theory."

"They can test the bones, can't they?" she asked, her voice shaky. "See if it's him?"

"I imagine they can, yes."

"I don't know if I want to know or not. I've sat here for fifteen years, listening for his truck coming up the driveway, hoping every time someone knocks that it will be him." Tears filled her eyes. "Randy and Jenna were what kept me going. And now with Randy gone..." She sobbed. "Thank goodness Jenna is pregnant. At least I'll have a grandchild."

I blinked at her. "What?"

She swiped at her eyes. "I'm not supposed to say anything about it; they're keeping it quiet. Please don't say anything to anyone."

"I won't," I promised, but that was certainly news to me. Before I could say anything else, Jenna and Simon walked into the kitchen; Jenna's eyes grew guarded when she spotted me. She wore a baggy sweater over slim jeans; if she was showing at all, it was camouflaged.

"What are you doing here?"

"This is Lucy Resnick. She brought fudge," Linda said. "And she says she thinks Chad may have been involved with those paintings they found at the courthouse."

She blinked. "Why does she think that?"

"I found a ticket tucked into the back of one of the paintings," I said. "It was from Houston, from a few days after your brother left town."

"Why would it be in one of the paintings?" she asked.

"We don't know," Linda said. "But it's more of a lead than I've had in fifteen years. I'm going to get in touch with the sheriff this afternoon," she said with resolve.

I hadn't had a chance to ask her any questions about Randy, and I got the sense that the moment had passed. Jenna was eyeing me warily—why, I had no idea—and her husband seemed anxious for me to leave. "We were just about to take Jenna's momma to town," he said. "Thanks for stopping by."

"Oh, it's no hurry," Linda said. "I'm thankful for the visit. And the fudge looks real good."

"Thanks," I said. "Oh... Rooster's out of commission right now, but if I were you, I'd get in touch with Deputy Shames. She's got a copy of the ticket already."

"We'll help you take care of that," Simon said. "Thanks so much for stopping by," he repeated, "but we're on our way out the door."

Message received, I thought as I stood up.

"I understand," I said, and then decided to throw one more thing out there. "Hey, I don't know if you know this, but a young woman who used to be Randy's girl-friend in high school seems to have vanished."

Jenna didn't flinch, but I could feel a change in the room from her and her husband. Her face remained impassive, but her eyes widened, and Simon's face twitched into a grimace before he smoothed it away.

"Who?" Jenna asked politely.

"Rhonda Gehring?" Linda asked. "She always was a flighty one. I was so glad Randy didn't marry her."

As she spoke, her eyes teared up. "She probably ran off with some other man."

"I'm so sorry to bring Randy up," I said. "I know this is a terrible time."

Jenna rushed over to her mother and gave me a nasty look. "Let me get you one of your anxiety pills," she said in a soothing tone. Jenna retrieved a bottle from the windowsill and tipped out a pill. "Maybe you need to lie down, Mother."

"I don't need to lie down," Linda responded in a tart voice, although she did take the pill.

"Well, then," I said as Jenna and Simon gave me icy looks. "It was nice visiting; I'm sorry to be the bearer of such difficult news."

Linda's eyes suddenly took on a teary sheen. "It is difficult," she said. "But somehow... I think I'd just sleep better at night *knowing*. All these years of wondering every night, trying to find out what happened... This is the first thing that tells me we might, somehow, find out at least something about what happened."

I didn't know what to tell her. All I said was, "I'm sorry it's been such a terrible trial, and that you've had to go through it twice. I hope you find peace."

"So do I," she said, and the grief in her voice was so raw it made my own heart hurt.

I made my way to the door with Jenna at my side; it was fairly obvious my presence wasn't welcome in the Stone household any longer.

"I'm sorry for your loss," I repeated.

"Thank you," she said with a tight smile as I stepped out the front door. "Goodbye," she said shortly, and shut the door.

Well, I thought to myself as I found myself alone on the front porch, Jenna and Simon seemed awfully anxious to get me out of the house.

I meandered down the front walk, pretending to stop and admire the boxwood that lined the walkway, and made my way toward the driveway. From there, I could see the guesthouse, a small building with shuttered windows. Was Rhonda there? I watched the house for a few minutes, looking for signs of life, but there was nothing.

With a glance back toward the big house, I drifted across the yard to the small building, pretending to be admiring the scenery. What I really wanted to do was knock on the door. I came closer, pretending to be interested in a rosebush planted at the corner of the small house, but really looking at the windows, hoping there would be some opening through which I could see what was going on inside. I had just bent down to "inspect" what looked like an antique rose when there was a thump from inside the house, and something that sounded like a chair being dragged along wood floors. Was Rhonda here? I was about to round the house when there was the sound of a door opening from behind me. I turned to see Jenna, standing at the back door of the main house.

"What are you doing?" Her voice was shrill

"I was just looking at the rosebush," I said pleasantly. "Is it an antique rose?"

"I have no idea," she said. "I think it's time you left."

"Sorry to intrude," I said, beating a retreat toward the barn.

She said nothing, just stood there watching me.

Tobias stepped out of the barn just as I got back to it. "How's the cow?" I asked, glancing back to where Jenna was still eyeing me.

"Healing beautifully," he told me. "I don't think I've

had a chance to introduce you. Lucy, this is William Stone."

"Nice to officially meet you," I said as the older man stumped out of the barn, his mouth set in a grim line. "I'm Lucy Resnick," I said.

"I saw you last night," he said shortly.

"I'm so sorry about your son," I said.

He nodded shortly, his eyes unreadable, then turned to Tobias. "She's good to go, then?"

"Just check on it and keep it clean," he said. "I might keep her in for a few more days, just to be sure, but there's no sign of infection."

"Good," he said. "Thanks for taking care of her. I'd better get on with my chores." He nodded a cool goodbye to both of us—he seemed fond of nodding—and disappeared back into the barn.

I waited until we got back into Tobias's truck to say anything. "Stoic," I remarked.

"He always has been. He's shaken up, though. I think he's saying as little as possible so he doesn't break down."

"I talked with Linda a little bit inside," I said as he backed up, "but Jenna and her husband were awfully eager to get rid of me."

"Did you tell her about the paintings, and the ticket?"

"I did. I didn't know how she'd take the possibility of the bones belonging to her son. I think she was upset, but also somewhat relieved that someone had found something that might explain what happened. It must have been awful, sitting for all those years and not knowing."

"What did she think of idea of the DNA test?"

"I didn't exactly bring that up, but I told her to talk with Deputy Shames. I think it's best for her to absorb things slowly; she's had a lot going on the past few weeks." I glanced behind me as the driveway curved to the right and the ranch disappeared. I thought again about Jenna and Simon, and how anxious they were to get me out of the house. There was something going on there, something they didn't want me to know. "Linda told me Jenna's pregnant, but that they're keeping it secret."

"She's pregnant?" he said.

"That's what Linda said. Why?"

"I heard through the grapevine they've been visiting a fertility clinic in Houston. I'm glad they found a solution."

"Molly did say something about that, now that I think of it. I'd forgotten." Good for Jenna, I thought. She hadn't been the politest to me, but that didn't mean I couldn't be happy for her. I knew the first few months were the riskiest; I wondered when she'd make the announcement. "I think someone is in the guesthouse, by the way."

"Jenna and her husband, or Rhonda?"

"Rhonda, I'm guessing; both Jenna and Simon were in the big house. I think they're hiding her."

"Her husband tends to be abusive; it could be she's hiding from him," Tobias suggested.

"Maybe," I said, "but I think something's going on. Jenna was quick to give her mom an antianxiety pill, and they hustled me out of the house fast." I glanced back at the house. "What do you think Simon's doing here if his job is in Houston?"

"Supporting his wife and her family? Plus, it's the holidays."

"You're probably right," I said. "I'm just desperate for the murderer to be anyone but Isabella. Or Mandy."

Tobias was silent for a moment. I looked out at the bleached winter landscape, feeling stymied. "Do you think Jenna might have killed her brother?" he asked.

"I don't know," I said. "I feel like there's something here I'm missing. I just don't know what it is."

"I'm sure you'll find out," he said. "You always do."

"Here's hoping," I said. I appreciated the encouragement, but I didn't share his rosy assessment.

Chapter 18

MANDY WAS HARD AT WORK at the *Buttercup Zephyr* when I turned up an hour later, butterflies in my stomach. As I walked up the front walk, I could see her through the window, staring hard at her laptop. She jumped when I knocked, and scurried to open the door.

"Lucy!" she said. "Did you find anything out?"

"I don't know," I said. I'd never seen Mandy look so exhausted and frazzled. Her hair was pulled back into a tight ponytail, dark circles ringed her eyes, and her face looked almost gaunt.

"Come in," she said. "I was just finishing the story on what happened at the Market last night. I can't believe someone killed Julie... she was so young. I still don't think it could possibly be true."

"I know," I said, feeling a bit relieved. She sounded genuinely upset.

"It's like someone has a vendetta against Rosita's," she said as she slumped back into her desk chair. "I need to talk to you anyway; you were there when they found her, weren't you?"

"I was. It was pretty shocking." I paused. "I was surprised not to see you there."

"I would have been," she said, "but I was trying to find the mayor. She got in touch with me about the ticket you found tucked into the frame of the painting; she was hoping I could find out more about it. Honestly, though, I'm still more worried about Isabella. Do you have anything new?"

"Nothing direct," I said, not yet willing to share. "Do you have any idea why anyone would have wanted to kill Julie? Did she and Randy know each other?"

"She worked at the restaurant, and I'm sure they interacted... she must have known something. Or seen something. That's all I can think of." She thought about it. "No. I have no idea."

"Did Randy hang out at the restaurant a lot?"

"When he and Isabella were in town, he liked to raid the cash register after hours," she said. "He'd go over and act like a business consultant to my parents. They were polite, but they just rolled their eyes behind his back."

"Nice," I said. "It's like he never grew up."

"Exactly. My poor sister," Mandy said. "I'm glad she won't be indicted for the second death, but I talked with Deputy Shames this morning, and apparently, Rooster's too busy trying to fix things up with Lacey to pay much attention to a murder investigation."

"Is she pursuing it at all?" I'd left her a message about what I'd learned at the Stones' house today regarding Sparky. I didn't expect anything to come of it—it wasn't like there was a last name or anything—but you never knew.

"She said she is, but who knows?" Mandy shrugged. "I tried to talk with Randy's sister, but she shut the door in my face."

"Why?"

"Because she thinks anyone associated with Rosita's is bad luck," she said. "I can see that."

"Maybe I can make some headway," I said, thinking maybe all my gift fudge might end up going to other causes. "Any other news?"

"Nothing," she said, looking hopeless.

"Where does Julie's sister live?"

"She's on the outskirts of Buttercup; her name is Caitlyn. She and Julie shared a trailer there."

"Do you have the address?"

"Right here," she said, reaching for a scrap of paper on her desk and handing it to me. "Let me know what you find out, okay?"

"Of course," I told her.

I pulled up outside Caitlyn and Julie's place less than a half hour later. The trailer, although old, was well kept, with a tidy wreath on the door and a small pot of pansies at the base of the steps. Although pansies meant spring to me, in Texas they were cool-season annuals; even after all these years, it was still strange to see their bright purple and yellow faces next to Christmas decorations.

A young woman I presumed was Caitlyn answered the door almost immediately, her eyes swollen from crying. She was wearing a worn bathrobe and pink socks, and her hair was piled in a loose bun that looked like she'd slept on it. "I'm so sorry to bother you," I told her. "I'm Lucy Resnick. I came to say how sorry I am about your sister, and to see if there's anything I can do to help." I offered her the box of fudge. She took it absently and waved me in.

Although the outside of the trailer was tidy, the inside was not. Dirty dishes had piled up in the sink, and clothes were piled on the back of the couch.

"The place is a mess," she said tonelessly. "I just don't have the energy."

"I understand," I said, sitting down on an empty spot on the couch. "Do you have family in town?"

"No," she said. "They live in the Valley... they're coming up tonight. I'm all alone now. I don't even know how I'm going to pay the rent now that Julie is gone." Her face crumpled, and she started to sob.

I hurried over and offered her a hug. She clung to me as if I were a life preserver, and I stroked her hair and murmured until the sobbing subsided.

"I'm so sorry," she said. "I'm just... not myself."

"Of course not. You just sit down there, and I'll make you a cup of tea," I directed, sensing she needed someone to take care of her.

She shrugged, which I took for assent. As she curled up in a chair, I put water on to boil and began tackling the mound of dishes.

"You don't need to do that," she said.

"I like to be busy," I said. "I'm happy to do it. In the meantime, if you're up for it, maybe you can tell me a little about your sister."

"Why?" she asked.

"As you probably know, the sheriff is a little bit occupied at the moment," I told her. "I used to be an investigative reporter in Houston. I'm hoping I can shed some light on what happened."

"You think you can find out who did that awful thing to Julie?"

"I can try," I said as I rinsed a plate and put it into the dishwasher. "Do you have any ideas?"

She shook her head. "I just have to think it had something to do with Rosita's," she said. "I mean, the first one happened in the parking lot, and Julie worked there."

I grabbed a handful of silverware and dropped it into the dishwasher basket. "Did she mention anything to you about anything she saw or heard at the restaurant?"

"She called me the night Randy Stone died," she said. "She was late coming home; she said they'd made her work overtime. She had to get off the phone quickly; she was a little preoccupied the next couple of days. Upset."

"Do you think maybe she saw what happened?"

"I don't know," she said. "She was just... upset about something. Maybe just that he died in the parking lot. I asked her about it, but she said it was nothing."

"Was she friendly with anyone in particular at the restaurant?"

"Not really," she said. "I mean, she was friendly to everyone, but no one she really thought was a friend. She didn't like Isabella much, though; she thought she was too bossy."

I wasn't surprised Julie wasn't a fan of Isabella. I imagine it must be hard to like the wife of a man you're infatuated with.

"Isabella just rolled into town about a month ago, and started coming in and telling everyone how to do their work; she made my sister scrub down all the bathroom floors just last week. Julie said it was disgusting." That sounded like the kind of job you'd give your husband's mistress. Did Isabella know about Randy and Julie? I wondered with a sinking heart. "It's just not fair... she was so young. She didn't do anything wrong!" Caitlyn rocked back and forth, hugging herself. "She'd only been working there a few months. She was going to go back to school for an accounting degree; we were sharing rent so she could save money."

"Did she have a boyfriend?"

Caitlyn shook her head. "I know she was interested in someone. I think it was someone at the restaurant. She was paying more attention to her makeup before she went in recently."

"Did she say who?"

"She told me I was imagining things," she said, "but I knew better. I don't know why she wouldn't tell me, though. Maybe if she had, this wouldn't have happened." Her face crumpled, and she reached for another tissue. After a moment, she wiped her eyes and took a deep breath. "I don't know. Maybe it was a customer or something."

"Or maybe it was someone who was married, or was seeing someone else?" I suggested.

"I wouldn't think Julie would do something like that," she said. I finished loading the last mug into the dishwasher and closed it, then reached for a sponge to wipe the countertops. "She was so focused on her future, on the life she wanted for herself."

"But you thought she was seeing someone."

"Or had a crush on someone." She was quiet for a moment. "Maybe she had a thing for Randy Stone. I was over there once, and he was really flirting with her."

"Was he?"

"It was about a month ago. He was a good-looking guy. I only met him once, but I could tell he was sleazy." Her eyes teared up again. "And now she'll never flirt with anyone again."

The teakettle whistled, and I rummaged around in the cabinets until I found some herbal tea. "Is chamomile okay?"

She nodded and dabbed at her eyes with a tissue. She'd been doing a lot of that; there was a pile of crumpled, mascara-stained tissues on the table next to her.

"I hate to ask this," I said as I put a tea bag into a mug and filled the mug with hot water, "but can you think of anyone who might have wished your sister harm?"

"No," she said, shaking her head vehemently. "I just can't imagine anyone wanting to hurt her."

I walked over with the tea and set it on the coffee table in front of her, clearing a space first. "And she never said anything about Randy Stone's death, or knowing anything about that?"

"No," she repeated. "Wait. She did say something about that night. That she never should have been there."

"What did she mean?"

"I don't know. Maybe she saw what happened to Randy. But why didn't she tell anyone about it?"

"That's a good question," I said.

Because if she had—if I'd waited at Rosita's five more minutes, or gone back to follow up—Julie might still be alive."

I stayed an hour, taking care of Caitlyn and listening as she mourned her sister. My heart ached for the poor family; no one should lose anyone to a violent death, and it was harder when the victim was so young. I left Caitlyn my card and told her to call me anytime; I made a mental note to ask Quinn if she knew of a good counselor who might work on a sliding scale. I was worried about Caitlyn, and glad her family would be in that night; I hated to leave her alone.

As the trailer receded in the rear-view mirror, I thought about the tangled web I was trying to unravel. Randy Stone was a smooth talker but a bad businessman... and wound up dead. The brother had disappeared fifteen years before. And then there was his sister, Jenna, and her husband. I didn't know much about Simon, only that something about him seemed familiar. And he had seemed a bit unsettled when I told him I had been a reporter in Houston.

Why?

As soon as I walked in the door, I went to my laptop and pulled up Simon Flagg's name. The first few entries showed him as partner in a development company in Houston, which was exactly what I'd expected to see.

But the third entry was something else entirely.

It was a story from a Houston news station. **LOCAL DEVELOPER SUSPECT IN WIFE'S DISAPPEARANCE**, it read.

Goose bumps rose on my arms as I clicked on the article.

The news story was from about ten years before. Apparently, Corinne Flagg had "just vanished" during a weekend in Galveston. She was supposed to visit a friend, but never turned up; the last time she was seen was with her husband. There was no further information in that article, so I clicked back and found a few more.

They all said essentially the same thing: that Simon and Corinne had been married for just over a year. Corinne came from a well-to-do family in the Dallas area. Together, they'd just purchased their first house and were planning on starting a family when Corinne just disappeared.

I scrolled through multiple articles. Over time, the

story had died. Corinne had never resurfaced. There were articles from time to time, appeals from the woman's parents to forward any leads, but no charges were ever filed and she was never found and, eventually, as I discovered from the Houston wedding announcements, Simon had remarried, this time to Jenna Stone.

There were a few more recent articles about Simon Flagg. His firm had taken a few hits. They'd been sued a couple of times, and had recently filed for bankruptcy. Which explained why the Flaggs were spending so much more time in Buttercup. There didn't appear to be a firm anymore.

Had Simon Flagg killed Randy Stone to make sure his wife inherited the ranch? Did he then kill Julie because she'd seen him do it?

If so, the real mystery remaining was why they were sheltering Rhonda Gehring at the guesthouse. Although I was starting to have some ideas about that, too.

I called the sheriff's office, but Deputy Shames wasn't there; Opal promised to have her call me as soon as she came on duty. Then I called Tobias: no answer. I put down the phone, not sure what to do next. I considered waiting before taking action, but I'd already waited too long once, and I didn't want another dead body. Serafine, after all, had warned that another death might be in the offing. After a moment's indecision, I picked up the phone again, left a message for Tobias telling him where I was going, gathered a few things, and then hurried out to the truck. Whether Jenna Flagg wanted me there or not, I needed to talk to Rhonda Gehring.

I didn't have an excuse for visiting the Stones—I'd already dropped off fudge—so I'd filled a little box of soaps and candles to take with me. If they caught me, I'd say I'd forgotten to drop them off earlier.

The gate to the ranch was open, so I drove in, hoping I'd be the only one around. I'd thought about waiting until evening, but if I was right about Simon, I wasn't sure I wanted to take the risk that something else would happen. Besides, I had a feeling the Stones were more the shoot-first, ask-questions-later type, and at least in the daytime, they'd be able to see who I was.

There were no cars in the driveway when I got there, thankfully. There was nowhere to hide mine, but I parked behind the barn so at least it wouldn't be visible to anyone coming up the driveway. What I was doing was dangerous; I was trespassing, and in Texas, that could be fatal.

I hurried over to the guesthouse, shooting furtive glances at the main house, and knocked on the door. I could sense movement from inside, but nobody answered. "Rhonda!" I shouted, knocking again. "It's important. Please open up."

Nothing... but I got a sense of waiting from inside the house. I knocked again: nothing.

I wasn't going to leave. I had to talk to her. So I did the obvious thing; I turned the doorknob and pushed, praying whoever was on the other side wasn't holding a loaded gun.

Chapter 19

THE DOOR WAS UNLOCKED, AND my instinct about the guesthouse's occupant was correct. She wasn't holding a gun; she was holding a spoon and a half gallon of Blue Bell Peppermint Ice Cream. "What are you doing here?" she asked. She wore sweatpants and a pink *Juicy* sweatshirt, and was brandishing the spoon like a weapon.

"I'm sorry to intrude," I told her, feeling adrenaline pulse through my veins, "but I think you may be in danger."

She blinked, looking like a twelve-year-old. "How did you find me here?"

"I saw you when I was here with Dr. Brandt."

"Oh, I remember. I stepped outside and heard voices. I'm not supposed to go outside at all, but it's so hard to stay all cooped up."

"Why can't you go outside?"

"Nobody's supposed to know I'm here. It's part of the terms..."

"Terms of what?"

She dropped her eyes. "Nothing," she said.

"I was worried about you when you left," I told her. "You could have left a note, you know."

"This isn't supposed to happen. I guess you'd better come in," she said. "Hurry, before they see you."

I stepped into the little house, and she shut the door behind me. "Come into the bedroom," she said. "Quickly."

"What are you afraid of?"

"I'm not supposed to tell anyone I'm here," she said, grabbing my arm and pulling me away from the door, dragging me into a small bedroom. "There," she said, peeking through the plantation shutters. "You have to leave. I can't talk."

"Why are you here?"

She rolled her eyes. "It's a deal I made. I can't talk about it."

"The six-month thing? Sadie at Shear Perfection thought it sounded fishy."

"You talked to Sadie?" she asked. "She wasn't supposed to say anything to anyone."

"I wanted to make sure you were okay. How did you get out of the farmhouse, anyway?"

"I called Jenna. She'd already talked to me. I left during the night and met her at the end of the road; she said she'd take care of me."

"Why did she say she'd take care of you?"

She backed away from me, and her eyes darted around the room.

"Tell me what it is, and I'll leave."

"No," she said, clutching the ice cream. "I can't tell anyone."

I sighed. "Look," I told her, "I think you're in danger here. Jenna's husband Simon was involved in the disappearance of his first wife. I think there's a chance he killed both Randy and Julie."

"Who's Julie?"

"She was a young woman who worked at Rosita's," I said.

"Why would Simon kill Randy?" she asked, a furrow forming between her tweezed eyebrows. "It's not like he was jealous of me or anything."

My eyes roved the room. The night table had a well-thumbed *People* magazine, an *Us* magazine, and what appeared to be an untouched copy of *What to Expect When You're Expecting*. "You're pregnant with Randy's baby," I said. "The Stones are going to claim it as their own so they can inherit the ranch."

Her eyes widened. "What? How do you know I'm pregnant?"

"I figured it out before I got here, but that kind of sealed the deal," I said, pointing to the book on the table.

"Oh, no," she said, turning pale. The carton crumpled a little in her hand. "What if they find out you know?"

"I'm not so worried about that," I said. "Here's the deal: I think Simon killed his ex-wife for money. I think he killed Randy so his wife would inherit the place. And I think he killed a waitress from Rosita's because she saw him do it."

"What? Simon…" She shook her head. "But even if that's true, why would he kill me?" she asked.

"You said it yourself; no one's supposed to know. What's going to happen after you have the baby?"

She dropped the spoon.

"I'm sorry to intrude this way," I said hurriedly, "but I was afraid they'd whisk you off to Houston and I wouldn't be able to find you. I know it's a cozy deal, but I think you should get out of here."

"You really think he'd do that?" she asked. "How do you know he killed the other people?"

"I don't have proof yet," I said, "but it fits. His development company in Houston just went bankrupt. They don't have any money. My guess is they're going to hang out and wait for Mom and Dad to die—if he doesn't help them along—and then he's going to just live off the profits of the ranch. If she fakes the pregnancy and your baby is Randy's, the child will be a genetic descendant of the Stones, so it will fill the bill in terms of inheritance."

Rhonda put down the ice cream, and her hands cradled her stomach. "He's really a murderer? My baby would be raised by a murderer?"

"I don't have proof," I said, "but wouldn't it be better to find out for sure before you commit to giving them your baby?"

"I don't want to die," she said. "I don't want my baby to be raised by a bad person. But if I don't take the deal, what do I do? I can't go home to my husband. I don't have anything. I'm not even sure I have my job."

"We can figure that out," I said. "And if it turns out I'm wrong, you can carry on. I promise I won't say anything to anyone; the inheritance thing is kind of silly anyway, to my mind. But for now, let's get you out of here."

She hesitated, then put down the ice cream carton. "Okay," she said. "Let me get my stuff."

As she spoke, there was the sound of a vehicle's tires crunching along the driveway. She sucked in her breath. "What if it's him?"

I hurried over to the window and peeked through the blinds. Sure enough, it was Simon, along with Jenna. As I watched, they both got out of the truck and walked to the house, where they closed the door behind them.

"Whew," she said. "You know what? Let me get my

stuff together and we'll go."

"Let's just skip the stuff," I said. "You didn't have much when you got here anyway. Grab your phone and let's get out of here."

"All right," she said. "I'll go."

"Is there a back door in this place?"

"No," she said. "Just the front."

I sighed. "I guess we'll have to risk it," I said. "My truck's out there; I'd say wait until dark, but the longer it's there, the more likely they are to find it. How did you hide here without Linda and William Stone finding out about you?"

"I was careful," she said. "I know his schedule. They haven't been in this guesthouse in forever; as long as I keep the lights off and don't go outside, they said I should be good. We were going to Houston in the next day or two, anyway."

"Glad I came when I did. Ready?" I asked.

She nodded, and I opened the door a crack. "Coast is clear," I said. "Let's go!"

Together, we ran out of the house. We were halfway to the truck when she stopped.

"What?"

"My phone!"

Before I could stop her, she ran back to the house and disappeared inside. She'd just made it back onto the front stoop when there was the sound of a door opening from the house, and Simon stepped out of the ranch house.

Rhonda froze, and her eyes darted to me.

And so did Simon's.

"Get back in that house," he said, his voice quiet and dangerous and absolutely terrifying.

"Come with me," I said.

"No," he said, and reached under his jacket. When his hand emerged, it had a gun in it. "Back in the house. Both of you."

Chapter 20

IN NO TIME AT ALL, we were back in the guest-house with the door shut behind us. I felt like a caged animal; adrenaline coursed through me, and I scanned the living room, looking for something I could use to defend myself. Although, against a gun, I wasn't liking my odds.

He turned the gun—and a disturbingly icy gaze—my way. "What are you doing here?" he asked, all the affability I'd seen before evaporating.

I swallowed, my mouth dry. "I came to see Rhonda."

"You told her you were here?" he said, swiveling the gun back to Rhonda. Her eyes widened; I could see the whites all around her pupils.

"No!" she said. "I haven't said anything to anyone. I swear!"

"She's telling the truth. I figured it out on my own," I told him. "I was coming to talk with her. That's all."

"You're trespassing," he said.

"I'm sorry. I really just came to see Rhonda."

"Why?"

"Because she disappeared from my house," I explained. "I was worried about her."

He said nothing.

"You know, other people know I'm here," I told him.

"But you won't be for long," he said. He turned to

Rhonda. "I wasn't supposed to take you to Houston until tomorrow, but I'm thinking we might have to take a trip today."

"Why?"

"You aren't very good at keeping secrets," he said. "I need to make sure you don't compromise us again. You knew the terms. I'm tempted to just call it off now."

"You can't," I said. "She's your only hope of a genetic heir. If you get rid of her, you lose your claim to the ranch."

His face hardened. "Enough," he said.

"What happened to your first wife?"

His jaw set, and he looked wary. "How do you know about her?"

"I'm an investigative reporter, remember? It must have felt so good to get rid of Randy. He was the only thing standing between you and Jenna's inheritance."

"Randy got what he deserved," he said.

Rhonda let out a small sob.

"And Julie?"

He shrugged. "A loose end. I don't like loose ends."

A chill ran down my spine. I was standing in the same room as a murderer. And not just a murderer, but one who dispatched his victims in cold blood. How were Rhonda and I going to get out of here?

"You killed him?" Rhonda asked in a tremulous voice. "You stabbed Randy in cold blood?"

"You're better off without him, I promise you," he said.

"Did you not see Julie's car at the time?" I asked. "How did you find out she saw you?"

"I wasn't sure. I knew he was with her. I saw the car in the parking lot that night. I staked out the restaurant at closing until I saw her leave. When she got into the car, I knew it was her."

"Why did you kill her at the Market?"

"Because there were so many other suspects," he said.

"You're a murderer," she said, as if by saying the words they would be easier to believe. "Was Lucy right? Did you kill your wife, too?"

He gave a slight shrug. "She had an accident. Things weren't going well between us. Plus, the life insurance policy helped with my business."

"Business isn't going so well right now, is it?" I asked, scanning the room for potential weapons. "That's why you're so interested in the ranch all of a sudden."

"We've had a few setbacks," he admitted.

"Bankruptcy's a setback," I said.

He let out an exasperated sound. "Enough talk. Where's your car?"

"My truck is behind the barn," I said.

"Where are your keys?"

"In my pocket," I said, reaching for them.

"No," he said, raising the gun a bit. "I'll get them." I cringed as he fished in my jacket pocket, pulled out the keys, and turned to Rhonda. "Gather all your stuff together."

"Why?"

"We're going to Houston today," he said.

She looked around. "But I don't have a suitcase. What do I put it in?"

"A trash bag. They're under the sink." He turned to me. "Help her."

That was just what I was hoping he'd say. I followed Rhonda into the guesthouse's tiny kitchen; as she reached under the sink, I bent down next to her. "Separate if you can," I said. "Different rooms."

She nodded, and we walked out of the kitchen with

Simon right behind us. "I'll take the bedroom," she said as I reached down to pick up the magazines from the end table.

He stood in the doorway of the bedroom, keeping an eye on both of us. I stuffed the magazines into the bag, along with the untouched book, then reached for a pair of socks crumpled on the floor next to the couch. There was still nothing I could find to use as a weapon.

I was slowly reaching for a book light when I heard a voice outside.

"Simon! Where are you?"

He swore under his breath. "Stay here," he said. "I'll be back to deal with you in a minute." He swung the gun around to cover both of us before sliding out the door. "I'm right here," he said, all the ice melted; back was the warm, generous voice I now knew was a total act.

When the door shut behind him, she turned to me. "What do I do?"

"Lock it," I ordered her. I already had my phone out and was dialing 911.

"But he'll be mad!"

"He's going to kill us anyway," I pointed out. "Might as well make it harder."

The dispatcher picked up as I finished speaking. "911, what's your emergency?"

I gave her a brief outline, along with the address, or at least what I knew of it.

"We'll send someone out."

"Please hurry," I said. "We've barricaded ourselves into the guesthouse, but he's armed, and we don't have weapons."

"We'll do our best," she said. "Do you want to stay

on the line?"

I turned to Rhonda. "Do you have your phone?"

She nodded.

"Call this number," I said, reeling off Tobias's cell number. "Tell him we're trapped here; see if he can get Deputy Shames to come."

"Okay," Rhonda said as she finished dialing.

"Ma'am?" It was the dispatcher.

"I do want to stay on the line," I said. If nothing else, at least it would be recorded. "But I think I'm going to have to put the phone down." I pulled the phone away from my ear and glanced at the battery; I had 30 percent left.

"Stay safe, ma'am," she said.

"He didn't answer," Rhonda told me.

"Leave a message," I advised, then turned my attention back to the dispatcher on the phone. "I'll do my very best to stay safe," I promised. I put the phone down and hurried over to push a chair up against the front door, wedging the top of it under the doorknob. "Are there knives in the kitchen?" I asked Rhonda.

She nodded, her eyes still showing white all the way around.

"Does the bathroom have a window?"

"It does," she said.

"Does the door lock?"

She nodded.

"Let's go in there, then," I said. "I'm going to grab a kitchen chair so I can brace it shut."

As I spoke, the doorknob rattled. Rhonda turned white.

"Does he have a key?"

"He does." Her voice was hoarse.

"Get into the bathroom," I ordered her. I ran into the

kitchen and grabbed a chair and a knife, then picked up my phone and slid it into my pocket. I could hear the dispatcher talking, but I didn't have time right then. By the time I got the bathroom door shut, I could hear him slamming his body against the door.

"He's going to kill us, isn't he?" Rhonda asked.

"Help me push this up against the door. We just have to stall him," I said, trying to sound encouraging. "Jenna's parents don't know about you, and Jenna doesn't know I'm here. It's an advantage."

Not much of one, for sure, but beggars can't be choosers.

Together, we shoved the chair up under the knob. "Will it hold?" she asked breathlessly.

"I don't know," I said. "Let's hope so."

"What do we do now?"

I pulled the phone out of my pocket. "We've barricaded ourselves in the bathroom, but he's about to break through the door. Any ETA?"

"They're on their way," she said. "That's all I know."

"Terrific," I said, just as the door to the guesthouse slammed open.

"He's in," Rhonda said in a voice that was almost a whisper.

I reached out and grabbed her hand. "The police are on their way," I reassured her.

I just hoped they'd get here in time.

❦

"Rhonda?" His voice was eerie, cajoling. "It's all gonna be okay," he said. "I don't want to hurt anyone. I just want to get you to Houston, so you and the baby will be safe."

She looked like she wanted to reply, but I held up a hand.

"Come on, sweetheart. You can trust me. I'm going to take care of you." We could hear his voice moving around the guesthouse. "Let's just make this easy, okay? If you come out now, I'll toss in an extra twenty thousand. Easy money," he said. "All you have to do is come out, and I'll take you down to Houston. You'll love the place. Jacuzzi tub, penthouse apartment... you'll be living in high style."

We could hear footsteps; all too soon, they stopped outside the bathroom door. "I know you're in there," he said. "There's nowhere to go. I have your friend's keys. Even if you could get out, it's a long way to the gate; you'll never make it."

I could feel Rhonda shaking beside me.

"Come on, just open up," he said. "I won't hurt you. I promise."

Rhonda couldn't resist anymore. "You killed the love of my life!" she wailed. "Why would I trust you?"

He swore, all the sweetness gone, and kicked at the door. The whole building seemed to tremble.

"Open the damned door!" he yelled. "I don't have all day. We just have to get this over with. I'm getting in there one way or another. Do you want to do this the hard way or the easy way?" He paused. "You won't like the hard way, I promise," he added in an ominous voice.

"Go out the bathroom window," I whispered to Rhonda while he talked. "Go get help from the house. I'll keep him occupied here."

"Are you sure?" she asked, eyes wide.

"I am. Go," I told her.

As Rhonda stood on the toilet and opened the window, I spoke. "Why did you kill Randy at Rosita's?" I asked to buy time.

"I knew he had a thing for a waitress there. He bragged about it to me. I figured it would be a good way to throw suspicion on someone else."

"And Rhonda's husband had just found out about the affair, so there were plenty of motives. Plus, with Rhonda pregnant, you had another opportunity. How did you find out?" I watched Rhonda; she'd gotten the window open and had put one leg through. I nodded encouragingly as Simon answered.

"Jenna saw her buying the test at the Red and White. When she found out about Randy and Rhonda, she reached out to her."

"So Rhonda called her from my house after her husband threw her out?" I asked as Rhonda got her second leg through. She let out a little "Oof" as she hit the ground, but Simon didn't hear her.

"She did. It was perfect timing."

Rhonda was out of the window by now. Her head popped up. "What do I do again?" she whispered.

"What?" Simon asked.

I cleared my throat. "I said, when is she due?"

"Six months, we think. She's got an appointment with a doctor in Houston next week."

As he spoke, I waved Rhonda to the main house.

"So you were going to bring the baby back here?" I asked, still buying time.

"That baby is going to be born with a silver spoon in its mouth."

"Will you be able to be a good father, knowing he or she isn't really yours?" I asked.

"Hopefully, the baby will have Jenna's good qualities, not her brother's."

"What if Chad comes back?"

"Oh, he died years ago," he said.

"How do you know?"

"I heard about the bones under the courthouse. I'll put my money on them being Chad's. But enough about family history. It's time for you to open that door."

"No, thank you," I said politely, praying Rhonda was able to do what I'd told her to.

"I hate to do this," he said, not sounding sincere at all, "but if you don't open the door, I'm going to have to kick it down. And if that doesn't work, I'm going to have to start shooting."

"If you do that, won't you alert everyone in the big house?"

"They're so hard of hearing they won't think anything of it. Plus, it's deer season. Now," he said, "are we going to do this the easy way or the hard way?"

I said a small prayer and climbed up onto the toilet, planning to follow Rhonda through the window. That was when the first shot sounded. Wood splintered, and the window shattered. Instinctively, I jumped into the bathtub and covered my head with my arms, curling up in a small ball and hoping it was cast iron and not fiberglass. As I did my best impression of a hedgehog, I could hear him trying the door, but it didn't sound like it was opening. A moment later, there was a second shot. This one seemed more effective; there was an explosion of wood shards, and I could hear the chair scrape against the floor.

He was almost in.

I made sure I had the hilt of the knife in my hand and stayed low in the tub as he further dislodged the chair we'd used to barricade the door. He kicked at the door again, and I could hear it slide further. I put the phone to my ear. "ETA?" I whispered, hoping the dispatcher was still there.

"Any moment, darlin'," she said. "You're doin' great."

The chair broke with a cracking noise; he was in. A moment later, Simon Flagg loomed over me, gun in hand. Was my last conversation on earth really going to be with the 911 dispatcher and a murderous lunatic?

I gripped the knife and was trying to come up with a desperate, last-ditch plan when a familiar voice sounded from behind Simon.

"Rhonda Gehring stopped in for a visit." It was William Stone. "She said you killed my boy."

Simon whirled around, still holding the gun.

"She's crazy," Simon said. "Always has been."

"She's not the one holding a Glock on a lady in a bathtub," William observed.

"She threatened me," he said.

"You're the one with the gun, looks like to me. I hear you killed my son and were going to try to pass his kid off as yours so Jenna would inherit the ranch."

Simon said nothing.

"I always knew there was something wrong about you. We would have died in our sleep real soon, isn't that right? And then who knows what would have happened to Jenna."

"You've got it all wrong, old man," Simon snarled. "This woman threatened me. I was defending myself." He raised the gun. "I recommend you stop pointing that thing at me, or I might have to kill you in self-defense."

"Just tell me straight," William said, his voice like iron. "Did you kill my boy?"

"I saved you from handing your life's work over to a

man who would have run it to ruin."

"Fine talk from a man who just filed for bankruptcy," he said. His voice was barely contained fury.

"Put the gun down," Simon said, advancing on him.

"You first," William said. "I don't want to shoot you. Well, actually, I do. But I'd really rather the law took care of things."

"I'll make it easy for both of us, then," Simon said, and shot William in the shoulder.

William staggered back, and Simon advanced.

I couldn't just let him finish it off. I leaped out of the tub and plunged the knife into Simon's gun arm.

"You stabbed me!" he said, as if he hadn't just shot an old man in the shoulder.

I put the knife to his throat. I had no idea what I was doing, but I wasn't about to stop now. "Put that gun down or I'll finish the job," I said in the coldest voice I could muster.

He started to move, and I pressed harder. A bead of blood showed at the edge of the knife.

"Fine," he said, and the gun clattered to the floor. William, in the meantime, had recovered, and was training the gun on his son-in-law.

"Get the Glock," he told me. I grabbed it from the floor and scrambled out of the bathroom to stand behind Simon.

"It was all for the best," Simon said, clutching his bloody arm.

"Not for us it wasn't," William said. "You stole my son. He wasn't always the brightest, and his business sense was a little underdeveloped, but he was ours. And now, thanks to you, he's gone forever." His voice shook; I could feel the grief pouring off him, and my heart ached for him.

A siren sounded outside. The cavalry, or at least the Buttercup Police Department, had arrived.

A moment later, Deputy Shames appeared at the door, with Tobias at her side.

"What's going on here?" she asked.

"It's a long story," William said, "but this man killed my son."

"We need an ambulance," Tobias said as he hurried over to inspect the older man's wound. Deputy Shames pulled out her radio and called for EMS.

I remembered my phone; I pulled it out of my jacket pocket and put it to my ear. "You still there?" I asked.

"I am," the dispatcher answered, "and I recorded the whole thing. And if I may say so, I'm awful glad that ended the way it did. It was touch-and-go there for a few minutes. You had me scared!"

"You're not the only one," I said. "Thanks so much for your help. I'm Lucy Resnick, by the way."

"Verna Robinson," the woman said. "Maybe now we'll get to meet in person sometime!"

"Let's plan on it," I said, my whole body suddenly feeling as limp as a noodle.

Chapter 21

JENNA AND HER MOTHER SHOWED up right after Deputy Shames cuffed a bleeding Simon.

"What's going on?" Jenna asked. "Why is my husband in handcuffs?"

"He shot me," her father said. "And he killed your brother."

"And Julie," I added. "And his former wife."

Jenna blanched. "What?" She looked at her husband, who appeared totally unabashed. "Is that true?"

"It was for the good of the family, Jenna," he said. "Randy would have taken everything that was yours. I was protecting you."

"Protecting me?" Jenna blinked. "Randy and I didn't always get along, but I loved him. He was my brother!"

"He was going to steal your inheritance," he said. "How could you love him?"

Jenna took a step back and took her mother's arm. Linda was pale; she looked to be in shock.

"Is there a blanket around?" I asked. "I think your mother needs to sit down and warm up."

"Oh, Mother... of course," Jenna said. "What was I thinking?"

Together, Jenna and I took Linda and sat her down on the couch in the living room. I grabbed a throw from the floor and draped it over her. "Is Billy going to be okay?" she asked in a faraway voice. `

"It was only a shoulder wound," I said. "Dr. Brandt is taking care of it until the paramedics arrive. He should be just fine."

"There was a lot of blood," she said. "So much blood. My two sons..." The tears came then, and Jenna hugged her. She, too, started crying.

"I'm so sorry, Momma," she said. "I didn't know he was bad. Honest, I didn't." She sounded like a little girl.

"He had us all snowed, honey," her mother said. "At least I still have you. And the baby," she said, eyeing her stomach.

"Oh, Momma. It's not me who's pregnant." Tears streamed down Jenna's face. "It's Rhonda. She's having Randy's baby."

Linda sat up straight. "What?"

"I hated to lie, but Simon said it was the only way.... I hope you're not too mad at me."

"Oh, sweetheart. I'm glad you and Simon weren't able to have kids; I don't want any of us to have any part of him around. But Rhonda... we'll have some of Randy with us, after all. And as for you, sweet pea... I think there will be children in your future. Just with a better husband. This may have been God's way of keeping you safe."

"It didn't keep Randy safe," Jenna sobbed.

"No," she said sadly. "It didn't." And she began to weep, too, the two women clinging to each other.

❦

I'd barely gotten back to the farm before the phone started ringing. I pulled off my shoes and ran to the phone; it was Mandy. "You solved it!" she crowed. "Isabella's free! You have to come to our family Christmas celebration. My mother and father insist; without you, our family might have been fractured forever."

I turned to look out at the driveway, where Tobias was parking his truck. "Can I bring a friend?"

"Of course," she said. "Come Christmas Eve. We always go to Midnight Mass, but you can skip that if you want to."

"Thanks so much for the invitation," I said. "Can I get back to you in a few?"

"Of course. And thank you, thank you, thank you!"

I hung up and looked at my ancient answering machine; it was blinking. I played the messages; the first was from Deputy Shames, telling me she had a lead on Sparky, and the second was from Fannie down at the antique shop. "Did you still want that vet kit? I've had a few inquiries, but I'll hold it for you if you're still interested." I quickly called her back and told her I'd be in for it tomorrow, managing to hang up just before Tobias arrived at the door.

Chuck and I went to greet him. I didn't throw myself at him, but Chuck was less reticent, and Tobias practically had to peel him off his pant leg.

"I'm so glad you're okay," Tobias said, pulling me into a crushing, warm hug. "When I got there, and saw the blood... I was afraid you were hurt. Or worse."

"I'm fine," I said. "I should probably change shirts, though." My sleeve was still damp with Simon's blood.

"I'll wait here," he said, sitting down and inviting Chuck up into his lap as I hurried to wash off my arm and change out of my ruined shirt.

"We never did talk about Christmas," he said when I returned in a soft, oversize sweatshirt.

"We didn't, did we? I just got an invitation for both

of us to go to a Christmas Eve celebration at the Vargases', if you're interested."

"I heard they throw one heck of a party," he said. "If
you're game, I'd love to go."

"I'd love to, also," I said, snuggling in next to him.
"It's been such a terrible day; I saw Julie's sister Caitlyn,
and she's absolutely devastated. I'm going to see if I can
get her some counseling; her parents are coming into
town tonight, but they're strapped for cash."

"I'll see what I can do, too," Tobias said. "We'll have
to keep an eye on her."

"I told her to call me anytime, but I'm going to
check up on her tomorrow." I sighed. "So many families have lost so much. I'm glad at least the Vargases got
somebody back."

"Death makes you realize how precious the people
close to you really are... and how fragile life is. I've
been thinking," he said, putting an arm around me and
stroking my hair. "I think I'm a bit afraid."

"Afraid?" I asked, feeling the warmth in my heart
suddenly chill.

"Yeah. As you know, my last relationship didn't end
very well," he said. "I just... I have such strong feelings
for you. I think I'm afraid to let my heart open up too
much."

"Really?" I asked.

"Really. I think I packed away a bunch of stuff after
my ex and I broke up, and I never really took it out and
looked at it. I think it may be time for me to change
that." He touched my chin and turned my head to face
him. "I love you, Lucy Resnick."

Despite all the tragedy of the day, my whole body
seemed to lift from the couch with joy. "I love you, too,
Tobias Brandt."

"I hope it's not too forward... but can I spend the night?" he asked. "Assuming Chuck approves, that is," he added, ruffling the fur on the apricot poodle's head.

"I can't think of anything I'd like better," I said, and he leaned down and kissed me. "Except maybe for that," I added a few minutes later when I came up for air.

It was the last night of the Christmas Market, so I put out all my remaining inventory, which wasn't too much. The Market was buzzing with the news of recent events... including Deputy Shames's discovery regarding Sparky.

"The Stone boy took up with an art thief," Mayor Niederberger said as she came by the stall. "Killed the boy off and put him under the courthouse... and then got himself killed in a shootout before he could come back to retrieve the loot."

"What?" I asked. "Where?"

"About six months later, in Chicago," she said. "A heist went wrong, and he got shot. If we hadn't done that renovation, no one ever would have found out what happened to the paintings... or to Chad Stone."

"Is the museum going to offer a finder's fee?" I asked.

"Fifty thousand is what they're sayin'," she said.

"That's a lot."

"Well, the paintings were worth five hundred thousand dollars," she replied, "so it makes sense."

"That'll help with the renovation."

"It will," she said. "Although I feel just awful for the Stone family. And for the family of that poor young woman from Rosita's."

"I talked with her sister; the family is devastated," I said. "Maybe some of the funds could go toward helping Caitlyn get some counseling, and to pay her rent."

"That's a good idea," the mayor said. "We'll see what we can do to help. At least they know what happened now, thanks to you," she said. "And Isabella will be with her family on Christmas, not sittin' in that cell rereading back issues of *Texas Monthly*."

"There's that," I agreed.

She bought two candles and drifted away a moment later.

A few minutes later, Rooster stumped by on crutches, looking grouchy, with a very tense-looking Lacey at his side. He wasn't at the deer lease, and I noticed they were both still wearing wedding bands, but it probably wasn't going to be the merriest of Christmases at the Kocureks' house, I thought as he scowled at me. I gave him a bright smile and said "Merry Christmas! I hope your foot gets better soon."

"Serves him right," Lacey said.

To my delight, the next family to arrive was the Stones. William was wearing a sling, but he seemed to be recovering nicely. Linda clung to his arm, and Rhonda and Jenna were talking in earnest a few feet behind them.

"So glad to see you up and around!" I said, smiling. "How are you all doing? I know it was a pretty traumatic day."

"We're trying to heal," William said. "We've decided we're going to have Rhonda stay with us until she has the baby. Jenna would like to adopt him... or her... but let Rhonda be involved as the baby grows up."

"That sounds like a great solution," I said.

"I'm going back to my job tomorrow," Rhonda said.

"I won't do the coloring, but I can still do cuts. I think Keith's going to file for divorce; I'm going to need to support myself."

"Take it easy, though, Rhonda," Jenna said. "It's been a rough couple of weeks."

"It has been for all of us," I agreed. "But it sounds like a wonderful arrangement."

"We're tickled pink," the Stones said. "Jenna's going to ease out of her job in Houston and come back and take over operations here. This little munchkin is going to have a big family taking care of her."

"She is." Rhonda smiled, her hand on her stomach. "Mmm. Those candied nuts smell delicious. I think I'm going to get myself some."

Jenna smiled, albeit a little bit sadly. "Of course. After all, you're eating for two!"

"First, though, I want to pick up a few things," William said. "Y'all hurry along; I'll catch up."

"Since when are you interested in soap and candles?" Linda teased him.

"Half the people on my shopping list are ladies," he reminded her. "Now, shoo!"

They headed toward the candied almonds, and he selected a half dozen soaps and four candles. "How much?" he asked.

I added it up and quoted a number. I used a candle to hold the check down so he could write it out, because he was short a functioning arm. When he was done, he handed it to me.

"Thank you so much," I said. "I hope you have a good Christmas after all; I know it's been a difficult month. Did you ever find out anything more about Chad?"

"It looks like that's who it is," he said with a grimace.

"They're doing DNA testing, but he broke his leg as a kid, and there's a healed fracture right where Chad's was." He let out a sad sigh. "After all those years of searching, I probably drove by my boy every day." Tears welled up in his eyes.

"I'm so, so sorry," I said softly. "I can't imagine. There's nothing worse."

"No," he agreed. "There isn't." He took a deep breath. "But we've got a new one on the way," he said. "I miss my sons every day—every minute, to be honest—but I'm grateful I have a daughter. And a grandbaby soon, too."

"I'm so glad," I said, smiling.

"I hear you're going to be renovating that old house you moved over to your place."

"Eventually," I said. "The bids are a bit higher than I'd hoped, to be honest, but I'll get there."

"You will," he said, picking up his pen and shoving another check under the candle.

"You've already paid," I said.

"I settled my bill, yes," he said. "But this is a gift."

A moment later, he handed me a check for ten thousand dollars.

"What? I can't accept this," I said.

"I insist you do," he said. "If it weren't for you, my daughter would have stayed married to her brother's murderer, and that young woman, Rhonda, might not have made it to next year. You saved our family... or what's left of it." His eyes teared up. "This is the least I could do, and I'm still in your debt."

"It's too much, though," I protested.

"Not if you're renovating an old house it isn't," he said. "And get that truck looked at. It's rattlin' something fierce."

"Are you sure?"

"I'm sure," he said, locking eyes with me until I accepted the check.

"Thank you," I said, my voice hoarse.

"And if you need anything—anything at all—don't hesitate to call."

"Thank you, Mr. Stone."

"Anytime, Ms. Resnick," he said, reaching out to squeeze my hand with his good one. "Now, then, I'd better make sure they don't buy out the whole nut booth. We've had enough nuts around the house already."

I laughed. "Thank you again," I told him before he left. "I can't wait to meet your grandbaby."

"Me neither," he said, grinning, and turned to rejoin his family.

Christmas Eve dawned, not with a dusting of snow, but with a cold breeze out of the north. The sky was a gorgeous, bright blue bowl above the farm, and after finishing my chores, I spent the day delivering gifts to friends and finishing up a batch of cookies to take to the festivities at the Vargases' house. I'd also given all the animals extra treats: carrots, apples, and even a few oats. Blossom nudged me with her nose, looking for more, and I gave her a kiss on her soft cheek. I looked down at the little house by the creek; thanks to the Stones, I would start renovations right after Christmas. And I hadn't fretted about the money I'd spent for Tobias's vintage vet kit.

Tobias showed up at five, looking handsome in khakis and a sports coat. The tree was decorated and twinkling in the corner of my living room, and Tobias's gift was wrapped and tucked beneath the branches, along with the gifts my friends had given me. I'd put on a red dress I hadn't worn since I left Houston, with a bit of red lipstick to match. With my new hair, I didn't look at all like Farmer Lucy. Except for my hands, which, as always, were callused, with short nails from lots of work.

"You look stunning," he said when I answered the door, Chuck leaping around his feet as usual. I'd given him some extra cheese and a cookie as a Christmas treat, and I had gotten a bone for him from the butcher at the Red and White Grocery.

"Thanks," I said. "You look pretty dapper yourself."

"Ready?"

"Let me get the cookies, and we'll go."

It was a short ride to the Vargases' ranch house, and Tobias held my hand the whole way. Several trucks and cars were already parked out front when we got there, and luminarias—paper bags filled with glowing candles—lined the walkway to the front porch. Christmas carols floated on the air, along with an absolutely delicious smell.

"What smells so good?" he asked as we walked up the candlelit path to the house.

"I don't know, but I suspect I'm going to want seconds."

Mandy answered the door, and before I could say anything, pulled me into an enormous hug. "You saved my sister," she said. "I can't thank you enough."

Isabella was right behind her. "Thank you so much," she said. "Because of you, I get to spend Christmas—and all the other days—with my family." She still looked bereft, but there was a spark of hope there I hadn't seen when I'd visited her in the jail.

"I'm so sorry about everything that happened," I said. "I know you and Randy weren't getting along, but it's still a real blow."

"It is," she said, and her eyes teared up. "I shouldn't miss him, but I do."

"Love's like that," I said, and gave her arm a squeeze.

Before she could say anything else, their mother, Valeria, came up and gave me a huge hug. "Here's the lady who saved my daughter! You are wonderful," she said, kissing me on the cheek soundly and squeezing me, then noticing Tobias standing beside me. "And this is your boyfriend?"

"Yes," I said happily.

"*Muy guapo.* And a vet, too?"

I could see Tobias blushing. "Tobias Brandt," he said, proffering a hand.

"Pleased to meet you. And please come in. You're our guests of honor tonight; you saved our family. We've got *ponche*, posole... and, of course, tamales!"

Tobias and I were greeted and hugged by all kinds of family members. The posole was amazing—rich broth with chunks of pork, garnished with radishes and greens—and the tamales, as always, were to die for. There was Mexican hot chocolate laced with cinnamon for the children, and alcoholic *ponche* for the adults, which, like everything else, was delicious, and went down almost too fast. After my second bowl of posole, Tobias grabbed my hand and pulled me outside to look at the stars.

"You can see the Milky Way," he said, tracing the pale streak across the sky with his finger. "I love the skies out here. Love it even more when I have someone to share them with." He pulled me close, and I leaned my head against his chest as I looked up at the sparkling night sky.

"It's so beautiful out here," I said. "I had a lot of fear about leaving my job and my life in Houston, but things have turned out even better than I could have imagined."

"Sometimes you have to take the risk," he said, and turned to me. "I do love you, Lucy Resnick."

"And I love you, too," I said, as he leaned down to give me the best kiss I'd ever received. "But I have a confession," I told him.

He pulled back and raised an eyebrow, looking wary. "Oh?"

"If you want a hand-knitted scarf from me for Christmas, you're out of luck."

He burst out laughing and then swept me into his arms. A moment later, together, we went back into the house, hands linked together, both filled to the brim with the spirit of Christmas.

MORE BOOKS BY KAREN MACINERNEY

To download a free book and receive members-only outtakes, short stories, recipes, and updates, join Karen's Reader's Circle at www.karenmacinerney.com! You can also join her on Facebook at facebook.com/AuthorKarenMacInerney and facebook.com/karenmacinerney.

And don't forget to follow her on BookBub to get newsflashes on new releases and sales!

The Dewberry Farm Mysteries
Killer Jam
Fatal Frost
Deadly Brew
Mistletoe Murder
Dyeing Season (Coming 2018)

The Gray Whale Inn Mysteries
Murder on the Rocks
Dead and Berried
Murder Most Maine
Berried to the Hilt
Brush With Death
Death Runs Adrift
Whale of a Crime
Claws for Alarm (Spring 2018)
Cookbook: The Gray Whale Inn Kitchen
Blueberry Blues (A Gray Whale Inn Short Story)
Pumpkin Pied (A Gray Whale Inn Short Story)

The Margie Peterson Mysteries
Mother's Day Out
Mother Knows Best
Mother's Little Helper

Tales of an Urban Werewolf
Howling at the Moon
On the Prowl
Leader of the Pack

RECIPES

GRANDMA VOGEL'S SNICKERDOODLES

Ingredients

Cookies
8 tablespoons (½ cup) unsalted butter, at room temperature*
¾ cup sugar
1 large egg
1 teaspoon vanilla extract
1 teaspoon baking powder
½ teaspoon salt*
1 ⅓ cups flour
*If you use salted butter, decrease the salt to ¼ teaspoon.
Coating
2 tablespoons sugar
1–1½ teaspoons ground cinnamon, to taste

Directions

Prehcat oven to 375°F and lightly grease (or line with parchment) two baking sheets. Beat together the butter and sugar until smooth. Add the egg, beating until smooth, then beat in the vanilla, salt, and baking powder. Add the flour, mixing until totally incorporated.

Make the coating by shaking together the sugar and cinnamon in a medium-sized zip-top plastic bag.

Drop small (1"-diameter) balls of dough into the

bag. Roll or toss the cookies in the cinnamon-sugar until they're completely coated.

Space the cookies at least 1½" apart on the prepared baking sheets, and use a flat-bottom glass to flatten them to about ⅜" thick; they'll be about 1½" in diameter.

Bake cookies for 8 minutes (for soft cookies) to 10 minutes (for crunchier cookies). Remove from the oven and cool them on the pan until they're firm enough to transfer to a rack to cool completely.

ROSITA'S TAMALES

Ingredients

3½ pounds pork shoulder or 3½ pounds pork butt,
*   trimmed of fat and cut up*
10 cups water
1 medium onion, quartered
3 garlic cloves, minced
3½ teaspoons salt
4 cups red chili sauce (see below for recipe)
¾ cup shortening
6 cups masa harina
1½ teaspoons baking powder
50 dried corn husks (about 8 inches long)

Directions

In a 5-quart Dutch oven, bring pork, water, onion, garlic, and 1½ teaspoons salt to boil and simmer, covered, about 2½ hours, or until meat is very tender. Remove meat from broth and allow both meat and broth to cool. Shred the meat using 2 forks, discarding fat, then strain the broth and reserve 6 cups.

In a large saucepan, heat the red chili sauce and add meat; simmer, covered, for 10 minutes.

To make masa, beat shortening on medium speed in a large bowl for 1 minute. In a separate bowl, stir together masa harina, baking powder, and 2 teaspoons salt. Add masa harina mixture and broth to shortening alternately, beating well after each addition. (Add just enough broth to make a thick, creamy paste.)

In the meantime, soak corn husks in warm water for at least 20 minutes; rinse to remove any corn silk and drain well.

To assemble each tamale, spread 2 tablespoons of the masa mixture on the center of the corn husk. (Each husk should be 8 inches long and 6 inches wide at the top. If a husk is small, overlap 2 small ones to form one. If it is large, tear a strip from the side.)

Place about 1 tablespoon meat and sauce mixture in the middle of the masa, then fold in the sides of husk and fold up the bottom.

Place a steamer basket in a large pot and put the tamales in the basket, open side up. Add water to pot so that the level is just below the basket. Bring water to boil and reduce heat. Cover and steam 40 minutes, adding water when necessary.

To freeze, leave tamales in the husks and place them in freezer bags. To reheat, thaw and wrap in a wet paper towel and reheat in the microwave for 2 minutes for 1 or 2 or resteam them just until hot.

RED CHILI SAUCE

Ingredients

15 large dried chilies (such as Anaheim, New Mexico, California, or pasilla)
4–5 garlic cloves
2 teaspoons ground cumin
1 teaspoon salt
2 teaspoons all-purpose flour
2 teaspoons olive oil

Directions

Remove stems and seeds from dried chili peppers, and place peppers in a single layer on a baking sheet.

Roast in a 350°F oven for 2 to 5 minutes or until you smell a sweet roasted aroma, checking often to avoid burning.

Remove the chilies from oven and soak in enough hot water to cover for about 30 minutes or until cool.

Put peppers and 2½ cups of the soaking water into a blender (save the remaining soaking water); add garlic, cumin, and salt, then cover and blend until smooth.

In a 2-quart saucepan, stir flour into oil or melted shortening over medium heat until browned.

Carefully stir in blended chili mixture.

Simmer uncovered for 5 to 10 minutes or until slightly thickened. (If sauce gets too thick, stir in up to 1 cup of the remaining soaking water until you reach the desired thickness.)

Note: When working with chilies, use rubber gloves to protect your skin, and avoid contact with your eyes. Wash hands thoroughly with soap and water to remove all the chili oils.

THE HITCHING POST'S TOM & JERRYS

Ingredients
3 eggs, separated
3 tablespoons powdered sugar
½ teaspoon ground allspice
½ teaspoon ground cinnamon
½ teaspoon ground cloves
4 ounces brandy, lukewarm
3 cups hot milk
Freshly grated nutmeg

Directions
In a large, clean bowl, beat the egg whites until stiff peaks form.

In a separate bowl, beat the egg yolks until light in color, then gradually beat in the sugar, allspice, cinnamon, and cloves. When thoroughly mixed, fold the yolk mixture into the whites. Pour 2 tablespoons into four mugs each. Add 1 ounce brandy and 1 ounce dark rum to each mug. Fill mugs the rest of the way with hot milk. Stir well, and dust with nutmeg.

ALMOND CRESCENT COOKIES

Ingredients

1 cup (2 sticks) butter, softened
½ cup powdered sugar plus more for rolling cookies
2 teaspoons vanilla extract
1 teaspoon almond extract
2 cups all-purpose flour
¼ teaspoon salt (not needed if your butter is salted)
1 cup finely chopped or ground almonds

Directions

Preheat oven to 325 degrees F. In a mixing bowl, cream butter, powdered sugar, vanilla extract, and almond extract. Blend in flour, salt, and nuts until dough holds together.

Shape dough into 1-inch balls and place 1-inch apart on baking sheets lined with parchment paper. Bake 15 minutes and until set, but not brown. Cool slightly, then roll in powdered sugar. Cool completely, then roll again in powdered sugar.

CANDY CANE FUDGE

Ingredients

2 (10-ounce) packages vanilla baking chips OR
   semisweet baking chips
1 (14-ounce) can sweetened condensed milk
½ teaspoon peppermint extract
1½ cups crushed candy canes
1 dash red or green food coloring (if using white
   chocolate… this is optional)

Directions

Line an 8-inch square baking pan with aluminum foil, and grease the foil.

Combine the vanilla chips and sweetened condensed milk in a saucepan over medium heat. Stir frequently until almost melted, remove from heat, and continue to stir until smooth. When chips are completely melted, stir in the peppermint extract, food coloring, and candy canes.

Spread evenly in the bottom of the prepared pan. Chill for 2 hours, then cut into squares.

CHRISTMAS PORK POSOLE

Ingredients

4 medium onions, divided
7 tablespoons canola oil or vegetable oil, divided
4½ tablespoons ancho chile powder, divided
3 tablespoons dried oregano (preferably Mexican),
   divided
1 6- to 6½-pound bone-in pork shoulder (Boston
   butt), cut into 4- to 5-inch pieces, some meat left
   on bone
5 cups (or more) low-salt chicken broth
4 7-ounce cans diced green chiles, drained
5 large garlic cloves, minced
4 teaspoons ground cumin
4 15-ounce cans golden or white hominy, drained
1 – 2 cups red chili sauce (see tamale recipe)
4 limes, each cut into 4 wedges
Thinly sliced green onion
Chopped fresh cilantro
Tortilla shells or chips, head of cabbage (chopped),
   5–10 radishes (thinly sliced), all optional for garnish at end.

Directions

Preheat oven to 350°F. Thinly slice 2 onions. Heat
4 tablespoons oil in heavy large ovenproof pot over
medium-high heat, then add sliced onions to pot and
sauté until onions begin to soften, about 3 minutes.
Add 1½ tablespoons ancho chile powder and 1½ tablespoons oregano and stir to coat. Sprinkle pork with salt
and add to pot. Add 5 cups broth. Bring to boil. Cover
and transfer to oven.

Braise pork until tender enough to shred easily, about 2 hours. Using slotted spoon, transfer pork to large bowl and pour juices into another large bowl. Refrigerate separately, uncovered until cool, then cover and keep chilled overnight.

Discard fat from top of chilled juices; reserve juices. Chop pork into ½-inch cubes, discarding excess fat.

Thinly slice remaining 2 onions. Heat remaining 3 tablespoons oil in heavy large pot over medium-high heat. Add onions and sauté until soft, stirring often, about 7 minutes. Add remaining 3 tablespoons ancho chile powder, remaining 1½ tablespoons oregano, diced chiles, garlic, and cumin, then stir 30 seconds. Add pork, reserved juices, hominy and red chili sauce. Bring to boil; reduce heat to low.

Cover pot with lid slightly ajar and simmer 30 minutes to allow flavors to blend, adding more broth to thin, if desired.

Ladle posole into bowls. Garnish with lime wedges, green onion, cilantro, and tortilla shells or chips, cabbage, and radish slices, as desired.

ACKNOWLEDGMENTS

First, many thanks to my family, Eric, Abby, and Ian, not just for putting up with me, but for continuing to come up with creative ways to kill people. (You should see the looks we get in restaurants.) I also want to give a shout-out to Carol and Dave Swartz, Dorothy and Ed MacInerney, and Bethann and Beau Eccles for their years of continued support.

Special thanks to the MacInerney Mystery Mavens (who help with all manner of things, from covers to concepts), particularly Alicia Farage, Rudi Lee, William Seward, Mandy Young Kutz, Kay Pucciarelli, Priscilla Ormsby, Olivia Leigh Blacke, Samantha Mann, Azanna Wishart, Norma Reed, Chloe Shepard, and my dear mother, Carol Swartz, for their careful reading of the manuscript. What would I do without you???

Kim Killion, as usual, did an amazing job on the cover design, and Randy Ladenheim-Gil's sharp editorial eye helped keep me from embarrassing myself. I want to give a big shout-out to the folks at Trianon, particularly Chloe, Ashley, and Stephen, for keeping me motivated (i.e. caffeinated) and being such terrific company. And finally, thank you to ALL of the wonderful readers who make Dewberry Farm possible, especially my fabulous Facebook community at www. facebook.com/karenmacinerney. You keep me going!

ABOUT THE AUTHOR

Karen is the housework-impaired, award-winning author of multiple mystery series, and her victims number well into the double digits. She lives in Austin, Texas with two sassy children, her husband, and a menagerie of animals, including twenty-three fish, two rabbits, and a rescue dog named Little Bit.

Feel free to visit Karen's web site at www.karenmacinerney.com, where you can download a free book and sign up to receive short stories, deleted scenes, recipes and other bonus material. You can also find her on Facebook at www.facebook.com/AuthorKarenMacInerney or www.facebook.com/karenmacinerney (she spends an inordinate amount of time there). You are more than welcome to friend her there—and remind her to get back to work on the next book!

P. S. Don't forget to follow Karen on BookBub to get newsflashes on new releases and sales!